THIRD CHOICE

DEBORAH WALLACE

Third Choice

Third Choice

Published by Deborah Wallace

Copyright © 2021 by Deborah Wallace

ISBN 978-1-951457-11-2

2/24, 8/24

Cover Art by Raymond and Deborah Wallace

Chapter 1

Susan put the phone to her ear, still staring at the contract she'd been reviewing.

"Sorry, Susan. This guy won't give a straight answer about what he needs to talk to you about. He's being kind of cagey," Jeannette said.

The secretary had been with the law practice for three years, but sometimes she was too soft-hearted when it came to clients.

"It's fine. Put him through." The phone clicked. "Susan Argyle."

"Good. I'm glad I got hold of you." The rough voice didn't belong to any client she'd had recently.

"Who is this?"

"Larry Proctor with the *Wilmette Ledger.*"

She huffed. "I don't do interviews. It's been six months. Isn't it about time this story got buried?"

"Mrs. Jeffers—"

"It's Argyle." She wanted to forget she ever had the last name of Jeffers. She'd kept her last name from her first marriage for her law practice, and hoped the notoriety would have died down after switching back to Argyle for her personal life as well.

"Ms. Argyle, I just want to find out if your life is getting back to normal since it's been six months since your husband died."

"Have you called anyone else six months after their husband died to ask how they're doing?" Silence was her answer. Of course, not. Reporters just called the wives of serial killers to see how they were coping. "Fine! I'm fine. And I'm even better if no one reminds me I married a crazy person. Goodbye, Mr. Proctor." She slammed the phone down, closed her eyes and pulled in a long breath, letting it out slowly. She rolled her shoulders, relieving some of the tension.

Susan picked up the phone. "Jeannette."

"Yes, Susan? Did I screw up?"

"You couldn't have known. Larry Proctor is a reporter. Don't take any more calls from him."

"Sorry. I won't. Oh, William Zimmer just called to cancel his appointment. Maybe you can leave early today."

Susan rubbed her forehead. "Thanks, Jeannette. I might just do that." She dropped the phone into the cradle. She rarely skipped out early, but a hug from Autumn would dim all the bad in her life.

She drove to the private school her daughter attended. About a third of the students stayed for the after-school program. She pulled her white Lexus into the only empty space, beside a red Ferrari. Ugh. If she'd noticed Abe's car while still on the street, she would have driven past and waited a few minutes before stopping at the school. The man was nice enough, and it was in his favor that he didn't judge her on her poor choice of her second husband. Maybe, if there'd been no Brian, she'd have been interested.

He and his daughter stepped out the door, and he paused when his gaze caught hers. A grin lit up his face.

He strode toward her, blocking her from continuing up the walk. "Susan, it's so nice to see you. I'm taking Tegan for pizza. Maybe you and Autumn can join us?"

Tegan was part of Autumn's circle of friends and they occasionally got together. The girls would enjoy the impromptu pizza party, but Susan wasn't up for it. She didn't want to encourage Abe. "Sorry. I've had a rough day. I just want to go home and relax."

He studied her face. "You do look tired. Maybe another time." Always hopeful, even though they'd never been on a date.

In this instance, she didn't mind the stresses of the day showing on her face. "Yes, maybe. It was good seeing you, Abe. Bye, Tegan."

The girl tugged on his hand. "Come on, Dad."

Susan stepped into the school building, stopped at the first room, a study hall, and peeked in. No Autumn, so she must not have needed help with homework. A few more steps brought her to a hum of childish voices in the cafeteria.

In the doorway, Susan scanned the kids, and zeroed in on Autumn. She sat with Heather and Grace. They whispered secrets between them and giggled. Her daughter's warm smile twisted her heart. It was so much like her father's. Anthony had been a happy man and even after six years, she missed his warmth and love. Sadly, most of Autumn's memories of her father were of how sick he'd been, and not the times before when he played with her.

Susan hoped he forgave her for the madman she'd brought into his daughter's life.

She wound her way through darting children and stopped beside the trio. "Hi, honey. You ready to go?"

"Mom! You're early. I was having fun." Her nine-year-old daughter was well adjusted despite the trauma she'd been through. She stood and Susan wrapped an arm around her. The girl gave her mother a quick hug.

This was exactly what she needed. "I am. We've got time for a swim before dinner."

"Yes!" Autumn picked up her books. "Bye, Heather. Bye, Grace."

Autumn chatted about a substitute teacher, which classmates were arguing, and everything else on the way home, while

Susan tried to keep it all straight. Some parents had to drag information from their children about school, so she was happy to listen.

She stopped beside the mailbox at the side of the road and collected the envelopes and the flyer for Not Just Trees Nursery. She glanced in the review mirror at the birdbath she'd picked up there that morning. Susan had seen their display of a birdbath reminiscent of a fountain in front of the inn in Italy where she and Anthony had stayed on their honeymoon. She bought it on the spot. After Theo and Bradley got home, she'd ask them to help her set up the fountain in the front yard.

Susan parked in front of her garage bay—the closest to the kitchen door of the four.

Autumn darted out, and moments later, she shrieked. Susan dropped the mail, scattering it over the front seat and floor, then raced across the lawn. Her daughter stood on the first step, sobbing into her hands.

Susan pulled her into a tight hug, and looked around. She shuddered and pulled in a shaky breath. On the porch, a huge, black-handled knife stuck straight up, skewering a folded paper and the body of a rabbit.

"Mom, somebody hurt it."

She pulled Autumn's head tighter against her. "Shh, honey. Let's get you inside."

Susan shook with rage and fear. Autumn didn't deserve this kind of torment.

They backtracked to the car and Susan hit the garage door button. She scanned the area but didn't see anyone watching. As soon as the door was high enough, Autumn darted inside, and Susan followed. She hit the button to close the garage door. In the utility room, she reset the security system then squatted in front of Autumn. "I have to call the police then we'll go sit in the living room."

She stood, and her daughter threw her arms around Susan. It broke her heart that Autumn had to suffer again.

A movement out of the corner of her eye startled her, and she tightened her hold on Autumn. Maybe the stalker had made it into the house.

"Oh, my!" The housekeeper clutched her chest. "Susan, you gave me a fright. I wasn't expecting you yet."

"Sorry, Miriam. I left work early today. We've had a fright, too." She gazed at her daughter. "Honey, can you go with Mrs. Devins into the living room?"

Susan walked across the room with Autumn and whispered in Miriam's ear. "There's a dead rabbit on the porch. I have to call the police."

Her eyebrows jumped up. "Yes, of course." She took Autumn's hand. "Come on, sweetheart. Let's go see what we can do in the living room."

After they left, Susan plucked her phone from her purse and scrolled through her contacts. "It's got to be in here."

Her shoulders sagged. There. Detective Wassman. She hit the button.

~~~

Detective Gary Wassman dropped into his chair and pulled up to the desk. He rubbed a hand over his head, leaving the short blond curls in disarray. Most of the other desks were unoccupied, the officers out on calls.

He was relieved he wouldn't be lead detective for the case he'd just worked. It was heartbreaking when a child's body was found. With the parents present, he'd gently questioned friends of the victim—witnesses to the abduction. Not something he wanted to do again, ever.

His cell phone chimed and he yanked it out of his shirt pocket. Not a number he recognized. "Wassman."

"Detective, I need your help." The voice sounded familiar, but he couldn't place it.

Gary grabbed the notepad on the corner of his desk and

picked up a pen. "Who is this and what can I do?"

"It's Susan Argyle."

That was the voice. It had grabbed him the first time he'd spoken with her. Auburn hair, deep blue eyes that he could have gotten lost in. Until they'd filled with pain when he'd informed her that her husband had been arrested on murder charges. He'd often thought about how she was coping.

"Can you come over? There was a…a…"

His chest tightened. "What happened?"

"A rabbit was…left on the front porch. With a knife stabbed into it."

"Are you inside now? With the door locked?" He stood and jogged between the desks, heading for the door.

"Yes. I'm kind of shaken up, as is Autumn."

"She saw it, too?"

"She saw it first."

"I'm sorry to hear that. I'll be there in ten minutes. Stay inside."

"We will. Thank you." She ended the call.

The poor woman didn't deserve this after all she'd been through with a husband who'd raped and killed red-headed women in her stead.

Once in his unmarked police car, he hit the siren and lights to cut the time in transit. Two blocks from her house, he shut them down and approached in silence. He pulled into the driveway behind Susan's car. He got out and scanned the area, not seeing anyone about, then he sprinted to the mansion's porch.

His gut churned at the sight of the grizzly remains that a child shouldn't have been subjected to. He snapped pictures from different angles, and close-ups of the hunting knife and pierced, folded paper. The rabbit was domestic—white with brown spots.

Gary collected a garbage bag, two evidence bags and gloves from his car. He donned the gloves and grabbed hold of the knife on the blade, next to the hilt, between his thumb and forefinger. He yanked, but it didn't come out. He ended up rocking the blade back and forth a few times. Whoever had done this had used a lot of force. It spoke of anger.

Blood smeared on the note as he slid it down the blade, but he figured it was best not to wipe the blade clean. Once the knife was bagged, he set it on the porch and opened the note. His breath caught. It was written in wide, black marker.

You're next

Murderer

He took a photo, then slipped the page into another bag.

The rabbit appeared young, not full grown. He took a couple of photos of it without the knife, then opened the garbage bag and draped it over the animal. He gripped the creature, and closed the bag around it, then sealed it.

He put the knife and animal in his trunk, removed his gloves, and skirting the blood on the porch, knocked on the door. "Mrs. Argyle, it's Detective Wassman."

A moment later, the door opened. Susan's face was as pinched as when he'd told her that her husband was the serial killer. And later when he returned to tell her the man had taken his own life.

He stepped through and closed the door. "I'm sorry this is happening to you."

"Shh." Her glance sliced to the side. Her daughter sat on the couch, her knees drawn up and arms wrapped around them. She watched them. A woman, with dark hair and a sprinkling of gray through it, sat behind Autumn. "Not too loud."

He gave a nod and lowered his voice. "Who's that with your daughter?"

"Our housekeeper, Miriam Devins."

"All right. I'll want to ask her some questions after we talk. Did you touch it?"

Susan shuddered. "No. I had to get Autumn inside. And even if she wasn't here, I wouldn't have touched that thing."

7

Susan's face paled, making her blue eyes seem brighter, when she spotted the paper in his hand. "What does it say?"

He pursed his lips, wishing he didn't have to show her, but it was the only way to figure out who had left it. Turning so the little girl wouldn't be able to see the writing, he held it out for Susan.

She gasped. "What's that supposed to mean? Does someone think I helped Brian kill those women?"

He wished he could take her hand. With everything she'd been through she needed a comforting touch. "I don't know yet. I'll do my best to get to the bottom of this. In the meantime, be observant of your surroundings. If you have a gut reaction that something doesn't seem right, heed that warning and get out of the situation."

Her eyes widened. "You think this isn't just a prank, but that I'm in danger?"

He hated worrying her. "This isn't like someone throwing eggs at your house. Someone killed that animal in anger. If anything more happens, call me. Even if you think it's nothing, I want to know."

She nodded. "I will."

"I'd like to check your locks to see how secure they are." It wasn't something he normally did, but he was concerned for her safety.

"We have a security system attached to all the doors and windows on the first floor." She patted the panel beside the front door.

"That's a start." He opened the door and examined the lock, noting the deadbolt was extra long. It was high quality. "Keep the deadbolt locked at all times."

She nodded. "We almost always do. I'll make sure from now on. I'll show you to the kitchen door."

On the far side of the kitchen, there was another door. Gary strode to it, finding a large mudroom behind it. A second security panel was on the wall beside a door. He opened it onto the garage. The lock was the same as the one for the front door.

He pointed at the large garage door. "Do you have a key-pad for entry?"

"Yes. And we all have our remote openers."

He patted the door beside him. "Do you keep this door locked?"

She bit her lip. "No. Because the garage doors are always closed."

A cold ball formed in his stomach. "That's not enough. Someone could figure out your door code, and there are devices that can send out random garage door signals. You've got four doors—four chances—that someone will hit on one that works."

Susan paled and her bottom lip trembled. "I didn't know. I'll tell everyone we need to lock this door, too."

"Good. Any other doors?"

Her chest expanded on a huge inhale. "Yes. In the pool room."

She led him in a labyrinth path to an Olympic size pool in a room big enough to hold a pool party. Two walls were floor to ceiling windows, with a set of French doors in each. A security nightmare.

She swept her arm. "All the windows and doors are wired. If there's a break-in, the alarm goes off and the police are notified."

He scanned the room, noting the security panel beside the door they'd entered. He checked the exterior doors—one in the center of a wall of glass and the other on the end wall—finding them as secure as all-glass doors could be. The side door led into a courtyard, maybe fifteen feet to the other wing of the mansion. Overhead, the roof was glass. The air conditioning must work overtime when it was hot. "Okay. I want to talk to your housekeeper, now."

They returned to the entry area. "Can you take Autumn into the kitchen while I talk with Miriam?"

"Sure." She went into the living room and held out her hand. "Autumn, let's go set the table for dinner."

After they left, Gary sat down near Miriam, and set the page facedown over his leg. "I'm Detective Wassman. Did Susan tell you what she found on the porch?" He figured the woman wouldn't want it repeated.

"Yes."

"Did you hear anything odd today?"

She turned her head to the side and back then sucked in a breath, her eyes widening. "Yes. There was this thump. I waited to hear it again, but it didn't happen, so I went back to work."

That must have been when the rabbit was stabbed. "What time was that?"

She rubbed the side of her neck with two fingers, her eyes unfocused. "It was after lunch. I was…changing sheets in Bradley's room. Front of the house. So, maybe around two-thirty."

"Good. That's helpful." Every bit of information might be of use. "Anything else?"

"No. I wish I would have thought to look out the window. I might have seen something."

"You couldn't have known. Keep your eye out for any other odd happenings. Here's my card if you notice anything." He handed one to her.

They stood and parted at the front door. Susan joined him. "Did she help you?"

"We've pinpointed approximate time."

"I hope that helps." Her hand touched the doorknob. Male voices drew his attention toward the kitchen. Two men, one dark haired, one light, walked into the foyer and stopped next to them—Susan's first husband's sons. They were a few years younger than her. Although the younger one didn't know it, he'd been on the suspected killer list for a short time.

"Detective, have you met my stepsons?" Susan asked.

"No, I haven't."

She waved her hand toward the dark haired man. "Theo,

Bradley. And this is Detective Wassman." Theo stood maybe an inch taller than his brother, with dark hair and brown eyes where his brother was blond and blue eyed.

Theo frowned. "Is there a problem, Detective?"

"Mrs. Argyle came home to a skewered rabbit on the porch." He held out the note. "Along with this."

Bradley swore and wrapped an arm around Susan's shoulders. A careful study of the men gave Gary the impression they were taken by surprise and worried for their stepmother. When he'd delivered his news of her husband's activity, then later, his death, they'd seemed supportive of her. Almost surprising, considering she'd married a killer a couple of years after their father had died.

From the start, Gary had thought the threat was aimed at Susan, but maybe not. "Is it possible this message was left for one of you?"

They shook their heads, and the blond spoke. "I don't think so, but I wouldn't have thought it was left for Susan either."

Gary looked Theo in the eye. "I didn't see any security cameras."

He sucked in a breath. "I'll call the security company immediately."

Gary gave a curt nod. "Front door, garage doors, and all that glass around the pool."

"Two days tops."

Although cameras wouldn't make the Argyles safer, they might help identify the stalker if he came back. "All of you keep an eye out for anything suspicious. Call me if anything seems out of the ordinary." Gary handed each man a business card, then stared into Susan's eyes. "Call me about anything that seems strange, no matter how small."

She bit her lip and nodded.

Gary went out the door, sidestepping the blood and damaged wood. He hoped one of the stepsons would clean it up.

11

He got into his car. His first stop would be getting the dead animal out of his trunk.

At the police station, he made his way to the medical examiner's office. It wasn't the right place, but he had no idea what to do with a dead rabbit that was evidence.

Gary pushed his way into medical examiner's office and held up the bag. "You want this?"

Sam Locke dropped his pen on the desk, and scratched the back of his head—a trait that made Gary wonder how the man wasn't bald in back. The rest of his dark hair was always neat.

Sam crossed his arms. "Probably not. What is it?"

"A dead rabbit. Skewered on a front porch."

"Why would I want that? I do autopsies not necropsies."

"Necropsies?"

Sam didn't often make him feel stupid.

"Autopsies on animals."

"Oh, uh. I thought you might be able to get some evidence from it." Not likely, but anything to figure out what this was about.

"Why is this so important?"

"It was on Susan Argyle's porch."

Sam tipped his head and squinted. "Who?"

"Jeffers."

His eyes widened. "The serial killer's wife?"

It bothered him that people thought of that first.

Sam stood. "Fine. Bring it to the autopsy room."

He followed the examiner into the cold room. All the tables were clean and empty. Thank God for that. He hated coming in when a cadaver's chest was pried open.

Sam pointed at the nearest table and flipped on a light. "Put it there."

Gary set the bag down, glad to be rid of it.

Sam pulled on gloves, untied and peeled the bag back. "It's young. I don't know rabbits, so I can't tell you how old. Domestic, of course." He wiggled the neck, and Gary shivered.

"Broken neck. My guess is, since there's not a lot of blood on the fur, it was dead before it was stabbed."

Gary shoved a thumb through his belt loop. "Do you think it was young enough it might have been recently purchased at a pet store?"

Sam shrugged. "Possibly. It's a start." He sealed the bag. "Do you want it back?"

Gary stepped back. "No. What am I going to do with it? Can't you dispose of it? And write up a report on it?"

"Sure."

"Thanks, Sam."

Gary dropped off the knife and note to the lab and filled out paperwork. Then he looked up pet stores that might sell rabbits. Maybe this stalker would have been stupid enough to buy it with a credit card.

Chapter 2

Gary struck out at the first two pet stores, who hadn't had rabbits for sale in months. He entered the third, Pet House, a medium-sized store with aisles of product. Birds chirped somewhere at the back, and puppies barked. He headed to the cashier, a pretty brunette barely out of her teens. No customers were nearby.

"Hi. Do you sell rabbits?"

She smiled. "Yeah. Over there." She pointed. "Just follow the wall until you get to them."

He found a picture on his phone he'd taken of the rabbit after he'd pulled the knife out. "I'm looking for this kind. Sorry. This one's dead."

She pinched her lips together and gave a nod then leaned over the phone. "It's an English Spot. We had some, but we're out. We'll probably get some more in a month or so."

"When did you sell the last one?"

A line formed between her brows. "Why?"

He pulled his badge from his pocket and flipped it open. "I'm investigating a case. Someone killed this rabbit and—"

She giggled. "You're investigating a rabbit murder?"

He grinned. "Not exactly. Can you tell me who bought this one?"

"No. Sorry. I could tell you what days the English Spots were sold, but the credit card sales don't match up to the purchases. And some were bought for cash."

He leaned a hip against the counter. "Would you or someone have given them names and could tell which one this is?"

She shrugged. "Maybe Katie could. She takes care of the animals."

"Is Katie here now?"

"Yeah, she's over there, cleaning puppy cages." She pointed in the direction of barking.

"Thanks."

Gary found a blonde with her hair in a ponytail leaning into a cage free of animals.

"Katie?"

She bumped her head as she withdrew. "Ouch!" She rubbed the spot. "Yes?"

He displayed his badge. "I'm Detective Wassman. I'd like to ask some questions about the rabbits." He held out his phone with the picture of the dead rabbit.

Her hand covered her mouth. "Traver. Is he…dead?" She blinked several times.

"Unfortunately, yes. I'm trying to find out who bought him."

"I hope you catch who did that. He was sold on my day off last week. Four English Spots were sold that day."

Too bad. This woman would probably have known who she handed each rabbit to. He pointed his thumb over his shoulder. "Was she here that day? And which day was that?"

"Amanda? I think so. It was Wednesday."

"Thanks." Gary worked his way back to the cash register and waited while the girl checked out a customer.

The man left with a bag of dog food, and the cashier turned to Gary. "Did she help you?"

"She said Traver was sold on Wednesday, her day off, along with three other English Spots. Were you working?"

"I must have been. We never get the same day off."

He laid his palm on the counter and leaned closer. "Did you help the buyers pick their rabbits?"

She shook her head. "Keith does that when Katie's not here."

"Okay. Then they come to your register."

"Yeah, but the animals are in boxes. Katie or Keith write the type of animal on the box. I don't see them except if they stick their nose or eye to one of holes."

This wouldn't be as helpful as he originally thought. "Do you remember anything about the people who bought the rabbits?"

Amanda closed her eyes and rubbed her forehead. "Not specifically. We had two kinds of rabbits. I remember a mother and daughter because the little girl was so excited. That's all I can tell you."

"Would Keith be able to narrow it down?"

She flipped her hand. "Pff. He just writes what's on the cage. He wouldn't pay attention to who he handed them over to."

Gary scanned the store, noticing two cameras. He pointed at the one aimed at the registers. "What about security cameras? Would there be a recording of those purchases?"

She glanced at the nearest one and leaned close. "We're not supposed to know, but the recorder doesn't work. The owner's a cheapskate. I'm sure he thinks customers will see the cameras and won't steal."

He let out a breath. That would have been too easy. He could rule out the mother and daughter. A woman wouldn't buy a rabbit for her child then take it away to kill it. Not that it mattered since he couldn't track the others anyway. Or maybe… "Can the owner match up sales with the credit cards by comparing dollar amounts?"

"I don't know. He's in his office back there." She pointed to a door at the back of the store.

"Okay, thanks. I'll try him."

Gary strode to the closed door and knocked.

"Come in," a muffled male voice said.

16

Gary opened the door and closed it behind him. "I'm Detective Gary Wassman." He flipped his badge open. "I'm trying to find out who purchased some English Spots over the last week or so. I'd hoped to match up the sales with credit cards."

The man shoved his glasses into place. "Sure. Let me see what I can find." He typed on his keyboard. "How far back do you want to go?"

Gary tipped his head. "Two weeks?"

"Okay. We only had this batch of Spots for about that long before they sold out. Before that, it was a couple of months ago."

"No, that's too far back."

The man typed again, and a sheet of paper rolled out of the printer. He snatched it up and set it down beside the keyboard. There were seven lines of text. "I've got the transaction numbers for the Spots." His fingers flew over the keys, and he used the mouse. A few minutes later, another paper rolled out of the printer and the man handed it to Gary.

"Here. I put it in a spreadsheet. The first column is the purchase date, the second is credit card number or cash, then customer name if it's a credit card, and the last is what they purchased."

"Thank you. You've been very helpful." Half the sales had been credit card. Likely, the rabbit in question was a cash sale, but Gary didn't have anything else to go on. He could be wasting his time.

But the 'gift' left for someone in Susan's house couldn't be ignored.

~~~

Usually, Gary felt satisfied after wrapping up a case, but not today. He'd spent two months investigating a burglary turned murder, and arrested the culprit that morning. His mind kept returning to Susan and the person behind the note that had been left two days before.

His desk phone rang. "Wassman."

"Hey, Gary. It's Dave. Got your results for the murdered rabbit."

Gary leaned forward, grabbed a pen and tapped it on the desk. "Tell me something good."

"Sorry. The perp must have worn gloves. Nothing on the knife. There's one smudge on the paper, but we couldn't get anything from it."

Gary's shoulders sagged. "Thanks for getting back to me so soon."

He set the phone into the cradle and opened the folder for Susan's case.

His boss strode past, grinning ear to ear.

"Hey, Luke. You're looking mighty happy."

Luke detoured and perched on the edge of Gary's desk. "Shannon stopped by and took me to lunch." He was still a newlywed after four months.

"I ate my lunch at my desk." He had way too many lonely meals. His last date had been before the serial killer case.

Luke's grin widened. "She couldn't wait until tonight to tell me she's pregnant."

"Congratulations. How do you think Sherry will take this?"

Luke's six-year-old daughter had loved Shannon from the start and called her Mom.

"She's been asking for a little sister since the wedding."

Gary chuckled. "I guess it's fifty-fifty that she gets what she wants." His gaze lit on the rabbit photo, and he frowned.

"New case?" Luke asked.

"Yeah. Susan Argyle has had a bit of trouble."

"Argyle?"

"Was Jeffers."

His eyes widened. "Ah. The wife."

If Gary could, he'd erase the fact that Susan had been married to that crazy scum. "Someone left her a message a couple of days ago, with a dead rabbit. 'You're next, murderer.'"

Luke squinted and rubbed his chin. "Do you think it was someone related to one of the women Jeffers killed?"

"No idea. I'll keep you apprised."

Luke nodded and stood. "Later." He headed to his office with a spring in his step.

Gary didn't know yet if this was a one-time incident. It could even be kids getting kicks, but they'd have to explain to their parents why the rabbit was missing.

He'd looked up addresses for the three names that used credit cards, and visited the homes. He'd felt a bit strange doing a bunny wellness visit, but all were accounted for. There'd been two who had used cash and that left him with a dead end.

He called up his notes on the serial killer case, and made a new list of the seven murdered women with names and phone numbers of family. The first had been a hitchhiker and they'd never discovered her identity. She had probably been his easiest kill—a chance encounter that started him on his killing spree.

Gary wasn't looking forward to questioning victims' families as to whether they were harassing the killer's wife. He was a pretty good judge as to whether someone was telling a lie, but he hated to approach people who had suffered such a loss. There didn't seem to be a gentle way to ask fathers and brothers if they held the killer's wife responsible for the death.

He'd start with Richard Lawson, father of the youngest victim. The man's office was nearby. Five minutes later, Gary parked in a space beside Lawson's building. He entered and the receptionist checked his ID then notified Lawson.

Mr. Lawson approached from a hallway and stopped in front of Gary. "Detective Wassman, what can I do for you?"

"May we speak in your office?"

Lawson's eyes narrowed. "All right. This way."

Once in the office, Lawson closed the door and took a seat with his desk between them.

Gary shifted in his chair. "How have you and your family

been doing?"

Lawson rubbed the back of his neck. "We're still recovering. My wife was hit the hardest."

"And your son?"

Lawson's mouth hardened. "John idolized his sister. They were close. She helped him with his homework and cheered him at all his games. It's been rough."

Gary wondered if Lawson was capable of harassing a woman who he might think contributed to his daughter's death. "Have you had any contact with Brian Jeffers' wife?"

"No. Why would I? It'd be painful for both of us."

The man seemed more puzzled at the question than anything else. Chances were Lawson wasn't responsible for stalking Susan. "Jeffers' wife has received a death threat that implies she's a murderer."

Lawson's eyebrows rose and he sat back. "Why are you telling me this?"

Gary shrugged. "I'm trying to find out who did it."

The man glowered. "I can't imagine any woman participating in what that man did to my daughter and the other victims. I wouldn't accuse her of being a murderer just because she was oblivious to his crimes."

"Good to know." Gary hesitated a moment. "Your son—"

The man rose. "What? You think my fourteen-year-old son would send a death threat to anyone? Yes, he grieves his sister's death, but he's too kind-hearted to do anything like that."

Gary asked a few more questions then stood. "I'm sorry I had to bring this up. Thank you for talking with me." He hurried to his car, glad one conversation was finished and not relishing talking to the man's son and the others. He had no problem questioning a suspected killer, but trying to find out if a victim's family member had murder on his mind made Gary uneasy.

He steeled himself to do it all over again.

~~~

Third day of talking to victims' families and it hadn't gotten easier. The hardest to this point had been talking to Richard Lawson's son. The boy had a hard time holding in his emotions. Gary hadn't sensed anger, just a wrenching grief. His mother had sat with an arm around the boy, her expression stoic.

Gary had chosen to visit Jordan Ford's boyfriend, Stewart Falcon, before the man left for work. He climbed the stairs to the second floor apartment and knocked on the door.

It swung open, and a man about his height leaned against the doorframe. His blond hair was damp, and only two buttons of his shirt were done. "I'm not interested in buying anything."

Gary flipped out his police ID. "I'm Detective Gary Wassman. I have a few questions."

Falcon's eyes narrowed. "What's this about?"

Gary glanced down the hallway. "Do you want to talk about it here?"

The man sighed and stepped back. "Fine. Come on in."

After Gary stepped inside, Falcon pushed the door closed, then crossed his arms. "I haven't done anything wrong."

Okay. So they weren't going to do this seated and Falcon already had his hackles up. He'd skip the niceties. "Brian Jeffers' wife has received a death threat that implies she's a murderer."

The man stuffed a hand in his pocket. "And this affects me how?"

Gary rested his hand on his belt. "Since Jordan Ford was your girlfriend, maybe you think Susan Jeffers was partially responsible for her death."

Falcon threw back his shoulders. "Maybe she could have been more aware of her husband's extracurricular activities, but I don't blame her for killing Jordan."

A little push might rile the man. "Been in any pet stores

lately?"

Falcon scoffed. "Seriously? I don't own pets. Why would I go into a pet store?"

"To buy an animal to kill?"

Falcon held his hands up. "Not me. I wouldn't do anything like that. I don't even hunt."

"Know anyone who would?"

"No. But if I come across anyone who would, I'll be sure to let you know."

"Where were you last Thursday afternoon?"

Falcon rubbed his chin. "Team meeting all afternoon. Ask my boss if you don't believe me."

Gary handed him his card. "All right. Thanks for your time."

Gary opened the door and strode away. Of all the men he'd talked to, Falcon was the most likely, although his protest seemed sincere. He was grasping at straws, but it couldn't hurt to print out Falcon's driver's license photo and show it at the pet store.

~~~

Gary entered Pet House and pulled Falcon's picture from his pocket. As last time, Amanda manned the register. He waited until two customers left and approached her. "Amanda?"

She squinted then smiled. "Detective. I didn't think you'd be back."

He shrugged. "Just following up." He held out the picture. "I know it's been a while, but do you think this man might have bought a rabbit?"

She took the picture, squinted at it, and bit her lip. "I don't think so. One of the guys was dark haired. The other..." She shook her head. "I don't think it was him. Sorry." She handed the page back.

"Is Keith in today?"

"Yeah. He's filling in for Katie."

"Okay. Thanks." Gary strode to the live animal area and found Keith boxing up a kitten for a customer.

The customer took the package and Keith turned to him. "May I help you?"

"I hope so." Gary held out the picture. "I wonder if you might recognize this man as one of the people who bought a rabbit week before last on Katie's day off."

Keith leaned forward, and shook his head. "He doesn't look familiar."

"Do you remember what the men looked like who bought rabbits?"

Keith rubbed his chin. "If you'd showed me a picture of a girl, I might remember, but a guy? No idea."

"Okay. Thanks." Gary tucked the picture back in his pocket. Showing Falcon's picture was worth a shot, but recognizing him hadn't been likely. He was back to square one.

~~~

A week had gone by since the rabbit incident, and except for Gary's weak suspicions of Falcon, none of his visits to victims' families had yielded any clues as to who had threatened Susan. The best thing that could be said was that he was done barging in on their grieving. His cell phone rang. The caller ID showed Susan Argyle. "Gary here."

Her anguish ripped through him. "Detective. It happened again."

"Another dead rabbit on your porch?" He was already on his feet, heading to his car.

"No. Someone axed my windshield."

"Where are you?"

"Murchison Law parking lot."

His gut cramped. "You're still outside? You're probably being watched. Go back inside until I get there." Someone could have kidnapped her as she stood beside her car. Since they hadn't, maybe they wanted to toy with her a little longer.

"Sorry. I didn't think of that." He didn't want to scare her, but she needed to realize the danger.

"I'll see you in fifteen minutes." The vandalizing of Susan's car proved that she was the target and not her stepsons. It wasn't a comforting thought.

He jumped into his car and called for backup to secure the scene. A squad car arrived right behind him. The parking lot was less than a quarter full. With all the employees who had left already, it was surprising no one had notified security of the incident. He parked near the entrance, got out and walked up to the police cruiser. "Can you find the car with the ax in the windshield and secure the area?"

"Sure thing, Gary."

Gary entered the building and found Susan talking to the security guard near the door. She looked shaken and pale, but otherwise all right.

Gary showed his badge. "I'd like Mrs. Argyle escorted to her car from now on."

Susan glared. "Detective—"

"This is serious. Don't take chances."

She crossed her arms over her chest. "Fine."

The guard—his ID said *Wayne M*—tipped his head. "I'll see to it."

"Thank you." He held out his hand. "Gary Wassman."

"Wayne Maguire." They shook hands.

"Do you have video surveillance of the parking lot?"

"Yes. But it doesn't cover the whole lot."

"Can I have a look at it for this afternoon?" It wasn't likely done in the morning or people going out for lunch would have seen it and notified the guard as they came back in.

Wayne led him to a small room in the corner of the lobby. "It's in here."

Gary followed him inside. The squad car sat at the edge of

one of the monitor screens and next to it was a car with a hatchet sticking out of the windshield. Not a great location for observation.

Wayne showed him how to operate the machine. "I've got to keep an eye on the entry door." He slipped out, but stood near the security room.

Gary ran the video in a fast reverse until a figure appeared. Once it exited the screen, he continued a few minutes more, then ran the video forward in normal time. No car had entered the lot in the short time before the figure had entered the screen. He must have come on foot from the back of the parking lot. The person wore a sweatshirt with the hood pulled up, and gloves covered the hands. The body appeared to be slim and of average height. After hitting the windshield a number of times, the stalker placed a paper under the wiper and raced out of sight.

There wouldn't be prints on the car, but maybe the perp had messed up and touched the hatchet without gloves.

He joined Wayne. "Can I get a copy of the video starting at three o'clock on sent to this email address?" He handed a card to the man.

The guard accepted the card. "I'll send it as soon as my replacement arrives in a half-hour."

"Thank you." Gary held the door open for Susan. "Let's drive my car over to yours." That way she wouldn't be standing around, exposed, while he collected the evidence.

They got into his vehicle, and he pulled up beside Susan's car on the opposite side from the police cruiser. One of the officers talked to two women who stood beside a sedan two rows over.

His blood boiled at the sight of the hatchet protruding from the windshield. She didn't deserve this.

Gary gathered a large plastic bag, an evidence bag and gloves. The ax head was buried to the handle on the driver's side. As he knew from the video, the vandal had hit the glass a few times before complete penetration. Someone had great strength or a lot of anger. A folded paper was jammed under the windshield wiper.

After numerous pictures, he removed the paper, opened it and took another photo, then slid it into the evidence bag.

Murderers

DIE

like he did

Since all Jeffers' victims had been female, Gary wondered if 'he' referred to Brian Jeffers. Did this person mean Susan should die since she was referred to as a murderer in the first note? For participating? For not stopping him? Or maybe she was a murderer because Jeffers' committed suicide and this person blamed her for his death.

He grabbed the ax handle near the head and yanked, then set it with care into the large bag so as not to rip it.

He debated about telling her what the note said, but his decision was taken from him.

Susan stepped from his car as he approached her. "What does it say?"

He held out the bagged note, and she covered her mouth. He hated the misting of her eyes and the pain it revealed.

He wanted to wrap an arm around her trembling shoulders. Instead, he gave her hand a squeeze. "Whatever this is about, it's misplaced. You're not responsible for any of it." What he wanted was for her to show anger toward the perpetrator for the vandalism and scare tactics.

She drew in a long breath and stood taller. "I know that in my head, but if I'd seen through him before we married, none of these deaths would have happened. Brad and Theo didn't like him. I should have trusted their judgment."

"Hey, you were married to their father. Of course, they'd be overly protective of you dating someone else. Besides, you weren't his first target he wanted to marry. He would have moved on, and someone else would have likely died."

She crossed her arms over her chest. "That doesn't make me feel better."

"Sorry. Do you want to call now for a windshield place to come fix it?"

"I guess I do have to call someone. I'll call our mechanic. He'll take care of it."

"Why don't you sit in my car while you do that?" He didn't want her exposed any longer than necessary.

He opened car door and directed her inside then stood beside her.

She pawed through her purse, brought out her phone, and dialed a number. "Hi, Mike. It's Susan Argyle." Gary couldn't distinguish the words on the other end. "Yes, I'm fine. Thanks for asking. My car's at work and the windshield is destroyed. Can you come pick it up?" More talking on the other end. "I'd really rather not go into it." She plucked her keys from a side pocket on her purse, and wound the car key off. "Okay. Under the mat, and you already know the door code." She tipped her head back and closed her eyes. "Thanks for rushing it, Mike. Bye."

He pointed at the officers. "I'm going to tell them to expect your mechanic." She nodded and he crossed to the men. "Mrs. Argyle has a tow truck coming for her car. I'd dust it for prints, but the security video showed the perp wore gloves. Can you two stay until he arrives?"

The shorter man replied. "Sure. No problem."

"Thanks." Gary returned to his car and slid behind the wheel. He couldn't get out of his head the way she'd talked with her mechanic. It sounded like a personal conversation rather than talking to a service person. It was crazy that he felt jealous. "It sounds like you know this Mike guy pretty well." He tried to convince himself that he only asked so he could rule the man out as a suspect.

"Mike? Yes. He's Bradley's friend. His dad died when Mike was fourteen. Anthony kind of became a surrogate father, so we saw a lot of him. He even paid for Mike to take auto mechanic school. Then when…" She closed her eyes for a few moments, and when she opened them tears misted her eyes. "When Anthony found out he was dying, he bought the perfect building for an auto shop. He added it to his will so that Mike inherited it and couldn't refuse."

Gary patted her hand. "Your husband was a good man."

"He was. We only had six years together, and he's already been gone five." She shuffled through her purse, found a tissue, and dabbed at her eyes. "I thought we'd have thirty more years."

Gary had read Luke's file on Jeffers and all the information about Susan. He'd always wondered why she didn't inherit when her husband died. Before meeting her, he thought Anthony Argyle had discovered his wife was a gold-digger marrying a man fifteen years older, and cut her out.

"How did you meet?"

A serene smile crossed her face. "I was out with friends at an upscale bar for my twenty-first birthday. Anthony was there with work associates. We kept eyeing each other, and one of the guys he was with goaded him into asking me to dance. We talked. A lot. He was impressed that I had already completed prelaw and was accepted into law school. We spent the rest of the evening together. There was never an awkward moment."

She closed her eyes and took his hand. He didn't think she realized she'd done it.

"And the rest is history?"

She chuckled. "Hardly. About a week later, he called and asked me out to dinner, said to dress up because it was a really nice place. I think he hoped I'd bomb, and he could forget about me. It was magical. I was so much younger than him, and he thought, for my sake, he should stay away, but he couldn't." Eyes still closed, she grinned. "It took six months of him trying to convince himself that he should leave me alone, but never succeeding for long. Finally, he gave in to the inevitable. We, um, got even closer. He proposed to me on my twenty-second birthday, and we got married a month later."

She opened her eyes and honed in on him. "And Autumn was born ten months after that." She jerked to attention. "Autumn! I have to pick her up."

Gary was disappointed when she pulled her hand from his. "I'll drive you. Maybe tomorrow, one of your stepsons can drop you at work. It's probably better if you're not alone anyway."

"Thank you. She's in an after school program on Belfort Court."

Susan had lost her one true love and then had been devastated by another man she'd loved. Gary had been attracted to her when he'd first met her months ago, but it didn't mean she was able to reciprocate. She wasn't ready to jump into another relationship—might never be.

Chapter 3

Gary sat in his car on the street outside Susan's office building. He was relieved she heeded his warning and had security walk her through the parking lot. This was the fourth day he'd watched and nothing was suspicious. If his intent was anything other than to keep Susan safe, he'd feel like a stalker. Three times throughout each day since the car vandalizing incident, he cruised the parking lot to make sure her car was unharmed. He hoped the person who terrorized her noticed him and gave up.

He followed Susan to Autumn's after school program and sat a block from the school as Susan collected her daughter. He didn't need to follow close to find his way to their house. Once they were safely inside, he headed home.

Gary parked in his garage and his cell phone rang. He glanced at the screen. "Susan, has something else happened?"

"No, Detective. I just wanted to tell you I noticed you following us, and although I appreciate it, it's not necessary."

"I feel more comfortable knowing you're inside and safe. And you can call me Gary."

Maybe he shouldn't have requested she use his first name. It made his protectiveness personal between them, and after her disaster of a marriage, she probably wasn't ready to think of another guy romantically. The first two times they'd seen each other had been related to her husband's murder charges. She certainly wouldn't have noticed him, but he'd sure noticed her.

Her strength when her world was falling apart had gotten to him. If her situation would have been different back then, he might have asked her out.

"Gary, you saw Wayne is walking me out, and I leave home the same time as Bradley."

It pleased him that she'd said his name instead of detective. "That leaves you at risk arriving home."

"It's not necessary to go above and beyond."

"I care what happens to you." Maybe he should have left it at going above and beyond, but he wanted her to know her safety was important to him. "It's no trouble waiting at your house to see that you and Autumn get inside safely."

"Okay. For Autumn's sake, I'll accept that. Bye, Gary."

"Have a nice evening, Susan." He understood her need to keep their interactions businesslike, but he hoped, given time, she'd see him as more.

If after a few more days nothing else happened, maybe whoever it was had given up on their bit of fun. Then he'd stop looking out for her. And he would miss seeing her, even if from a distance. Nope. He wasn't stalking.

~~~

Susan waved to Gary as she turned into her driveway. It was sweet of him to go out of his way to ease her fears like this. Maybe the scare fest had ended, and sadly, she wouldn't see him again. A week had passed since the last incident.

She pushed the garage button and the door rose, allowing her to pull into her space—the closest of the four to the kitchen door. The third space, Bradley's, housed his Porsche since he rode in with Theo. As the door descended, she caught a glimpse of Gary's car driving by.

She and Autumn were safe inside.

"Mom, can I have a snack?"

"Honey, we'll be eating in a half-hour." Autumn pouted

and Susan hid her smile. "Mrs. Devins made a treat for dessert."

She unlocked the mudroom door, and reset the security system. She hated the extra step, but the importance overrode her resistance. She entered the kitchen behind Autumn. A tantalizing tomato and herb aroma made her stomach growl. "Now, wash your hands and set the table, please."

Susan headed to the front door to check the mail, having been too distracted by Gary to collect it. She opened the door and smiled at the new fountain. It sat halfway between the porch steps and the road. Theo had complained about the weight as he and Bradley set the base in place. Then they'd huffed as they carried the top. They'd had to figure out the best placement for the solar panel that powered the fountain motor, but it worked perfectly.

She stepped onto the porch, stunned by the litter in front of her. Cut up yellow roses lay over a sheet of paper and on the porch, partially obscuring the large, black letters on the page.

He gave
YOU
Flowers

She slammed and locked the door, then dropped her forehead against it. She'd hoped it was over. At least someone hadn't killed another animal or vandalized her car again. She straightened her spine, retrieved her phone from her purse, then pressed Gary's name.

"Hey. Is everything okay?"

It took a couple seconds to find her voice. "No. Can you come back?"

"Give me three minutes."

"Thank you."

"Mom, I'm done setting the table."

Susan couldn't break down in front of her daughter. She pulled in a long breath. "Thanks, honey. Why don't you finish your homework in the living room until your brothers get home?"

"Okay. Can we swim after dinner?"

"We'll see."

Autumn made a pouty face, then ran toward the kitchen to get her bag. Susan peeked out the front window as Gary pulled into the driveway and parked in front of her garage door. She waited until he came up the front steps before opening the door.

Gary glanced at her. "I'm sorry this is still happening to you." He pulled out his phone and snapped a few shots of the mess on the porch. "Let me get bags for these."

If the stalker had left a bouquet, Gary would probably have seen it from the road, but these shredded petals, leaves and stems lay almost flat on the floor.

He jogged to his car and returned with evidence bags tucked under his arm, then he pulled on gloves. Gary tipped the paper and the flower pieces slid into a bag, then he gathered the scattered remaining pieces. Someone had cleaned the blood away from the rabbit incident, but the gouge from the knife remained. He hoped Susan wasn't the one who removed the stain.

"I don't think we'll get anything useful from the flowers, but I'll give them to Dave, our forensic specialist, anyway."

He took a picture of the page before slipping it into a second bag. The gloves snapped as he pulled them off, then stuffed them into his pants pocket. He stared at the black words a few seconds before turning it to face her. "Funny how 'you' is all caps, like this person wanted flowers and didn't get any."

"I didn't think of that. Brian used to give me flowers. They were *always* yellow roses. Do you think the color is a coincidence?" She hated talking about her husband. She couldn't even call him ex because he hadn't given her a chance to divorce him before killing himself.

He shook his head. "No idea. When did he give you flowers?"

She shrugged. "Birthdays, our anniversary, Valentine's Day. Every few weeks near the end."

His eyes widened. "Every few weeks?" It was as if he'd latched onto something.

Her breath hitched. "Is that important?"

"Not really. I just wonder if…"

"If what?" She didn't like his hesitation.

He tipped his head up for a couple seconds, then stared her in the eyes. "If he gave them to you after each murder."

She covered her mouth, a shiver of revulsion skittering up her spine. "I don't know. Maybe. But it doesn't matter now, does it?" She hadn't had a perfect marriage, but before Brian's arrest, she thought they'd loved each other. He hadn't gotten along with his stepdaughter, but she'd thought, given time, they'd become friends.

He shrugged. "No, it doesn't matter. It's more my detective's curiosity." He tapped the paper. "Back to this. Do you think he had a jealous lover?"

"I wouldn't have thought so, but as it turns out, I didn't know him at all." She'd never guessed anything was wrong. People still looked at her as if she should have known he was a killer.

"I noticed the security camera. Can we check the feed?"

Theo had kept his word. The cameras had been installed two days after the first incident.

"Yes. The company put in a new panel by the back door, but I don't know how to make the video play."

"Let's go have a look."

Bags in hand, he followed her to the mud room then she stepped aside. He stared at the panel for a minute then pushed some buttons. She only knew the picture was reversing because the time display changed. A figure appeared on the screen, and when it disappeared again, Gary tapped a button and it played at normal speed.

34

The figure strode across the lawn, wearing a sweatshirt with the hood up and head bowed. One gloved hand held a plastic bag. First the paper was pulled out and set on the porch floor, then the bag was upended and the shredded flowers rained down. The figure balled up the bag and stuffed it into a pocket, then hurried away.

Susan sighed. "I didn't see anything to identify him. Did you?"

He shook his head. "No. He was careful. Either he knew the camera was there or he was overly cautious."

Gary took out his phone, glanced at the panel and punched in a number. "Hi, this is Detective Gary Wassman. I need you to send me the feed from this afternoon for the Argyles." He read off the number on the panel. "Yes. Send it to me at the station. Thanks." He gave his email address.

He slipped his phone into his pocket and rested his hand on her shoulder. The warmth began to chase away the chill. It wasn't an impersonal touch. It seemed as if he knew she needed the contact, and the concern in his eyes warmed her more.

"That's all I can do right now."

His hand dropped, and the chill invaded her insides again. "Thanks for coming back." She followed him to the front door and locked it after he left. Too bad that didn't block out the fear.

~~~

The next morning, Gary studied his copies of the three notes spread side-by-side on his desk. He scrawled on them what they'd been found with and the date of the occurrence. Usually, stalkers escalated, but the last note was tamer than the first.

His boss strolled through with a cup from the local coffee shop in his hand.

"Hey, Luke. Got a minute?"

Luke hooked a sharp right, sat on the corner of Gary's desk, and took a sip of coffee. "What's up?"

"This Susan Argyle stalker thing doesn't make sense." He waved at the pages on the desk. "What order would you put these in?"

Luke flipped them around, and re-ordered them with the flowers first, 'you're next' second, and 'murderers die' last.

Gary tapped the note that had been covered in flowers. "I thought the same, but this one showed up yesterday with cut up roses. Yellow ones. The same color Jeffers always gave Susan." He touched 'YOU'. "This sounds like a jealous lover didn't get flowers, but knew what color Jeffers gave to his wife."

"Sounds possible."

Gary leaned back. "The first two messages, I thought, were written by a man accusing Susan of contributing in some way to the murder of a loved one. Especially, adding in the dead rabbit and hatchet. I even interviewed all the men related to the victims."

He tapped the flowers message. "But the third has me re-thinking. This sounds like a woman who loved Jeffers. Before or after he married Susan—I don't know that it matters. Maybe she blames Jeffers' suicide on Susan. He killed himself right after she refused to provide a lawyer. In this woman's twisted mind, maybe that means Susan killed him."

Luke nodded. "I agree that killing a rabbit and swinging an ax sound like a male stalker." He tapped the word 'flowers'. "But this changes everything. Why don't you try to find Jeffers' old girlfriends?"

"I did that when I investigated him for the serial killer case. All I came up with were rich women he dated for a short time, and they all ended the relationships." He sure wished Susan would have been one of the temporary girlfriends instead of the wife. Jeffers had swooped in while she was vulnerable after her first husband's death.

In a sense, he was doing the same. Because of this stalker,

she was vulnerable again, and he was making a move. *He* wasn't the same though. Gary cared about Susan and wanted the best for her.

Luke sipped his coffee. "Did you investigate his family? Maybe one of them knows about a serious girlfriend who's not one of the wealthy women."

Gary narrowed his eyes. "It seems like he didn't have much family, but I'll recheck it. And maybe I'll hit some out-of-town bars with his picture. I might get lucky and find someone who saw him with a woman." Over six months after the last killing, chances were slim that witnesses would remember seeing Jeffers, let alone with a woman.

Luke tapped the desk with his knuckles and stood. "Looks like you've got your work cut out for you."

As Gary shuffled the notes into a pile, the dates jumped out at him. He checked his calendar. They were one week apart on Thursdays. He'd have to be extra vigilant the next Thursday.

The flowers. Maybe a florist might remember who bought the roses. He looked up local shops and found two. He dialed the first.

"Plantopia."

"This is Detective Gary Wassman. Do you sell yellow roses?"

"Yes. I think we have a dozen left."

"Have you sold any in the last two days?" He hoped it could be this easy.

"Yesterday to a regular customer. He has a standing order for once a month."

"All right. Thank you." No way could that man have destroyed the flowers on Susan's porch. He hung up and dialed the other number.

"Underwood Florists."

"This is Detective Gary Wassman. Do you sell yellow roses?"

"Not at the moment. But we've got red, white, and pink."

"Have you sold any yellow in the last couple days?"

"No. Someone came in and bought all five dozen…let me see…four days ago."

"Okay. Thanks."

A florist was out unless the stalker had gone out of town for them. Then he remembered the grocery store he shopped at carried flowers. Maybe they had roses, too. He'd check on his way to the bar.

He called up a map program on his phone and plotted a dozen bars to visit. He caught up on paperwork while waiting for mid-afternoon. Since Susan hadn't known about a girl-friend, Jeffers probably met her during work hours.

At two o'clock, he headed out. His first stop was the gro-cery store. He was surprised to find dozens of yellow roses. No way would anyone remember one person who bought some, likely mixed in with their groceries.

Disappointed, he continued to the first bar on his list. He'd struck out at five before he had to head back. He'd gotten a list of employees who'd been off that day and intended to go back and interview. Gary doubted he'd find anyone who had seen Jeffers with a woman.

From the last bar, he went directly to Susan's office in time to follow her home. He kept his distance and waited until she was inside before driving away. Duty had nothing to do with his efforts.

Once, a few months after he'd made detective, Gary had a stalker case. He hadn't thought it was as important as a murder case he'd been working on and didn't put as much time on it as he later felt he should have. He worked on it, trying to track down witnesses to the notes left for the victim, but it hadn't been the first thing he did each day. That was a mistake he wouldn't make again. The victim had disappeared, and after five years was still missing. His priorities flipped then. A live victim was more important than one who was already dead. Except in serial killer cases, the murderer wouldn't likely kill again.

Now, Susan was his number one priority. He'd do his best to make sure nothing happened to her. She'd become more important to him than any previous cases.

~~~

Autumn was asleep and Susan had the rest of the night ahead of her. She pushed deeper into the overstuffed chair and held her phone. Her gaze traveled over the room that she'd shared with Anthony. She'd moved back into the suite after finding out Brian had killed those women. She'd had nightmares, but they would have been worse sleeping in the bed she'd shared with a serial killer. She might have considered moving, except Autumn would have missed Theo and Bradley too much. She couldn't take her away from their love and a stable home.

She shivered. All Brian's victims had red hair like hers. Every woman he raped and murdered were her effigies. She'd asked Anthony to give his money and property to his children in his will, and he'd grudgingly agreed, except he'd insisted on giving her a generous allowance for as long as she lived. If she'd inherited part of the estate, the women wouldn't have died. Brian would have killed her to inherit her share of the money, and that would have been the end of it. No other deaths.

Except if Brian had killed her, it wouldn't have been the end for Autumn. Susan's daughter would have grown up an orphan. She wished she'd heeded Autumn's dislike of Brian. She'd thought, over time, they'd grow to like each other. But no. He'd tolerated her and Autumn ignored him.

Then there were Anthony's sons. Bradley had been ambivalent about Brian, but Theo had hated him. They'd rubbed each other wrong on first meeting, and it had grown worse over time. After she married Brian, they'd probably said no more than a handful of words to each other. Susan sighed, wishing she'd had Theo's perception.

Anthony had been loving and caring. Susan had thought she'd found the same in Brian, but he'd fooled her—the lonely, vulnerable widow. Again she was alone, but she hoped not so vulnerable.

Now she had to decide if she was willing to take a risk with Gary. He seemed to honestly care. Not many men, even policemen, would have followed her to keep her safe. She was sure this case and his job didn't require him to monitor her movements. It was his concern that pushed him, but except for a few glimpses, he'd kept their relationship professional.

Those times where it was more personal, her heart had fluttered. She'd been able to forget for a few minutes the reason he was present.

It would be up to her to take the first step. Too bad she didn't know what to say. There was a reason she went into real estate and contract law. She didn't have to sway juries. She dragged in a long breath, and whooshed it back out. This was ridiculous. She was acting like a school girl with her first crush.

Susan pressed Gary's name in her contact list.

"Susan. Are you okay?"

She knew this was a bad idea, but now she'd taken the plunge and couldn't back down. "Um. Everything's fine. I…just wanted to talk." She closed her eyes and shook her head at sounding like a teenager.

"What about?"

A band tightened around her chest, making it hard to breathe. "Maybe this was a bad idea."

"Why don't you tell me how your day went?"

The pressure in her chest eased, and she let out a breath, hoping it didn't sound like a sigh. "I helped a young couple close on their first house."

"Do you like doing house closings?"

"It's all right, but I love closings like I had today." She tipped her head back and stared at the ceiling. "The husband was trying to be serious and mature, but his wife couldn't sit still in her seat. She's six months pregnant and was so excited about moving into their own home before the baby's born."

"That's nice."

"After we finished, she gave me a hug, and the husband shook my hand. I couldn't resist peeking out the window. A few steps down the walk, he picked her up and kissed her." She sighed. "They were so sweet."

Gary chuckled. "I remember how excited I was when I bought my house."

"I wished I experienced my first home-buying experience, but Anthony had lived in our huge house for a decade before we got married. For a long time, I felt like an interloper."

"It must have been difficult moving into a ready-made family."

She grinned. "You have no idea. I'm five years older than Theo. It was more like the boys were getting an older sister instead of a stepmother."

He laughed. "If I recall how I was in my teens, I'd be pretty hot for the beautiful college student who moved in."

Susan pressed a hand to her warm cheek, pleased he thought she was beautiful. She wondered if he was hot for her now or only that his teenage self would have been. "It took nearly a year before they accepted me. We became friends."

"I'm glad you have that. It would have been difficult to live with ill feelings."

"Fortunately, they never hated me. They were more wary than anything. Since Anthony died, they treat me like a sister."

"How's it been since…Brian?"

She gripped the edge of the chair cushion. "They never liked him, but they didn't treat me any differently. Since he…died, they've been extra sweet to me. I couldn't have gotten through this without them."

"Good. You deserve support."

"And Autumn, too. They're wonderful big brothers." She yawned. "I should let you go. Sorry I talked your ear off."

"No, you didn't. It would have been a dull evening without your call. Are you sure everything's okay?"

"I'm better now." She'd enjoyed their talk, too. "Goodnight, Gary."

"Sleep well, Susan."

She dropped her phone in her lap. She'd done it—had a conversation with Gary that didn't include the terrible messages left for her. His voice had been soothing with a hint of sexy. The times when he laughed, she wanted to be right there with him and give him a kiss.

She didn't know precisely what drew her to him. Tegan's father, Abe, was more attractive in a GQ way, but he left her cold. She couldn't wait for the next glimpse of Gary. His big shoulder muscles would have no trouble picking her up. She never thought she'd find someone again who made her overheated, but Gary did it with a look or his voice over the phone.

The only thing she regretted from her conversation with Gary was not finding out more about him. Next time. And maybe he would be the one to call her.

Chapter 4

During the next few days, Gary interviewed employees at the rest of the bars on his list, returning to talk to missed employees. He'd come up empty. Back at the office, he drew up a list of a dozen more bars to visit. It probably wouldn't do any good, but he had no other leads right now.

Most detectives would have taken statements and put little time into investigating the dead rabbit incident, at least until the hatchet hit the windshield. But from the first, Gary hadn't brushed it off as nothing. Some serial killers had started their 'careers' by killing animals when they were children. He couldn't say that the person harassing Susan was a serial killer, but he or she seemed to have no qualms about killing—animals anyway.

Gary read through his notes for Jeffers' serial killer case. The killer's father died when Jeffers was eighteen, and his stepmother died when he was twenty-three. His half-sister was five years younger than him, but it hadn't seemed important to try to track her down at the time. Callista Jeffers would now be twenty-five. He searched the department of motor vehicles in her parents' home state for her address and came up empty. She must have moved away.

It was possible that without any other family, she'd lived close to Jeffers. A search of the local motor vehicle drivers' records revealed nothing. He wondered if Susan knew anything about her. He'd carry out more research tomorrow.

It was time to make sure Susan got home without incident. He waited across from her office. She left the building, deep in conversation with a different guard. He couldn't help but feast on her shape in a wine colored skirt that hugged her hips. He followed her car to Autumn's school, then to their house. Once she and Autumn were safely inside, he headed home.

Gary whipped up a stir-fry while soft classical music played from the living room. He enjoyed the meal as he got lost in a sci-fi book. After dinner, he settled into his favorite chair to continue reading.

Evenings were usually quiet. Sometimes he met up with a few colleagues from the station for a beer, but he hadn't done that for a couple of weeks. He didn't want to miss a call from Susan while in a noisy bar.

He'd read two chapters when his phone rang. Susan. It was around the time she called last time, so he was pretty sure it wasn't an emergency. He set his book beside him, and grinned.

"Hi, Susan."

"Hi, Gary. How was your day?"

He chuckled. She'd started the same way he'd gotten her talking. "I ran into a lot of dead ends today."

"That's too bad. Does it happen often?"

He tipped his head back. "More often than not. Detective work is following a lot of leads that go nowhere or that uncover tiny pieces of the puzzle."

"Is that my case or another?"

"Two cases, but I spent the most time on yours."

"So you're saying you haven't found out anything about who's leaving these messages for me?" She sounded disappointed. He couldn't blame her. He was, too.

"I'm no closer to figuring it out than I was at the beginning." He wished he had good news for her. "Oh, do you know anything about Brian's sister?"

"Sister? He told me his parents were dead. He never mentioned a sibling, so I assumed he was an only child."

"No. He has a younger half-sister. I was hoping to ask her some questions about possible girlfriends Brian might have had, but I haven't been able to locate her yet."

"Sorry I can't help."

He sat straight. "Hey, did he ever tell you about any ex-girlfriends?"

She snorted. "I never thought about it at the time, but pretty much all I knew about him was that his parents died, and things about his golf career."

"That's all right. I'll find what I need." He hoped. She hadn't called to talk about Jeffers, and Gary wanted to make sure she knew more about him than Jeffers had told about himself. "I hope your day was better than mine."

"I did research, and it went well. Friday, Autumn is going to a sleepover at a friend's house. I, uh, wondered if you wanted to come to dinner at the house."

He hadn't expected Susan to take the first step and he was pleased. "Are you sure?"

She gave a nervous chuckle. "Yes, but I have to warn you. The boys—" she laughed "—their dad always called them that. Anyway, Theo and Bradley will be there. And umm, with my poor judgment of Brian…"

"You want their approval before we go any further?"

"Yes. Do you mind?" Her tone sounded hopeful.

"I understand completely. I don't mind. And thank you for asking me on a date." He hoped *the boys* approved, because he was pretty sure that if they didn't, he'd have to work that much harder to prove himself before getting another chance. He'd start by not calling the CEO and VP of a billion dollar company boys.

"You're calling it a date?"

"Sure. Why not? We're having dinner together."

"With my stepsons! But thank you. I'm glad you're not letting this sort of test scare you away." That answered his question of if she was ready to date again.

"Not at all." It did unnerve him a bit, but he'd pay the price. It would be worth it if he got Susan to fully trust him. And she did trust him a little or she wouldn't have made the first move with that initial phone call. He understood her doubt in her own judgment.

They talked twenty minutes more, then Susan yawned. "Sorry. I really have to get some sleep."

"I didn't realize how late it was. I enjoyed talking with you. Pleasant dreams, Susan."

She yawned again and laughed. "You, too. Goodnight, Gary."

He wouldn't be falling asleep anytime soon—not with his worries over not passing her test.

~~~

As Gary sat at the curb waiting for Susan to leave the office, he drummed he his fingers on the steering wheel. It was Friday, and he was looking forward to staying when they reached her house. One good thing happened, or hadn't happened, that week. Thursday came and went without her getting another message.

Susan strode out of the building with Wayne by her side. She waved at Gary.

He'd stopped making multiple trips through the parking lot throughout the day, but every night when he arrived, he always circled past her car to ensure nothing had happened to it. If possible, he wouldn't let her experience a similar trauma alone.

Susan pulled her car into the street, and Gary followed behind. At her house, the garage door opened, and he turned into the driveway, parking behind her space.

She stepped out of her car. "Come on in this way."

"Hold on a sec. I want to check your front porch." It was possible no one had come out onto the porch, and a *gift* had sat all night. He paused a few feet from the steps, and inspected the area in front of the door. Nothing.

He strode into the garage where Susan still waited. "I had to make sure."

She gave a quick nod. He wished he hadn't spoiled the moment and hoped the whole evening wasn't ruined.

Standing close to Susan at the entrance door, he caught a floral scent, and wished he could bury his nose in her hair. She hit the button with the number one above it, and the garage door closed. She unlocked the door. He was glad she followed the safety suggestion he'd made. She led the way into the house, pushed the security buttons, and entered the kitchen.

He drew in a long breath. A savory beef scent filled his lungs. "That smells fantastic."

She smiled. "I can't take credit for it. Our housekeeper, Miriam, keeps us well fed. I just have to serve it."

He raised his brows. "Even weekends?" He'd love to come home to cooked meals after work.

"We're on our own for Saturdays and Sundays. We take turns. Theo is by far the best cook. He used to cook with his mom."

He followed her into the kitchen and washed his hands at the sink. "What's your go-to meal to make?"

Susan took four plates from a cupboard and set them on the counter. "Beef stew. I can get all the ingredients into the crock pot by noon and turn the broth into gravy just before we eat." At the cupboard beside it, she pulled out four tall glasses. "I usually also make biscuits."

"That sounds really good." Gary picked up the plates. "Where do you want these?"

"Hold on." Susan raided the silverware drawer and set forks and knives on top of the plates, then picked up the glasses. "This way."

He followed her into a dining room. She set glasses at four places on the long table, and he added the plates and silverware. No one would be sitting at the head of the table. From a china cabinet drawer, she grabbed burgundy cloth napkins and placed them beside each plate.

Male voices entered the kitchen, and he only now wondered if Susan had told Theo and Bradley he would be joining them.

The men entered the dining room. Susan had told him Theo looked very much like their father, and Bradley favored their mother. He strode forward and stretched out his hand. "Good evening, Detective."

Gary shook both men's hands. "You can call me Gary. Nice to see you again, Theo. You too, Bradley." Neither seemed surprised he was there.

"Susan, I'll help bring in the meal," Theo said.

Gary took a step to follow them. "Can I help?"

Theo waived him off. "We've got it."

Now that Gary stood alone with Bradley, his heart rate kicked up a notch. Maybe having a couple of dates before a family dinner would have made him more comfortable, but this was for Susan's peace of mind.

"You're the one who told Susan that Brian had been arrested, and the next day told her he'd committed suicide."

It wasn't a question and not a comfortable way to start a get-to-know-you conversation. "Yes. She was unbelievably strong."

Bradley shoved his hands into his pockets. "Until after you left. Then she fell apart."

"I'm glad she had you and Theo to support her. She said the two of you are like brothers to her."

He chuckled. "We never thought of her as a stepmom, that's for sure."

Bradley pulled his hands from his pockets and squared his shoulders. "So here's my protective brother routine. Susan was naive when she married Dad. Bubbly and trusting and so in love. Which was fine with Dad because he was crazy about her. She was totally unprepared when Brian swept into her life. Too trusting. She was still recovering from Dad's death, and she couldn't see the real Brian."

It was no surprise Susan garnered this kind of loyalty. "She told me how the two of you tried to dissuade her from seeing Brian."

Bradley's eyes widened. "She did, huh?" He held his hand out to shake. "Okay. I'm giving you the benefit of the doubt. But if you hurt her, I hurt you. Even if you are a cop."

Gary grinned. "Thank you. I have no intention of hurting her. But if I do and you beat me up, I won't press charges."

Bradley laughed and slapped him on the back. "I think I like you."

He'd won over one of the brothers. Hopefully, it was a sign of how dinner would go.

"Step aside." Theo swept into the room with a full tray, and Susan followed, carrying a water pitcher.

She poured water into their glasses.

"Let me get wine," Bradley said. He headed into the kitchen.

Theo slipped a platter of some kind of sliced beef wrapped around mushrooms onto the table, as well as bowls of broccoli and whole red potatoes.

Bradley returned with a bottle and four wine glasses. He poured the red liquid into the glasses and set them at each plate. "I should have recognized that scent when we came in. Mushroom stuffed flank steak. It's been months since Miriam made it." He clapped Gary on the shoulder. "You're in for a treat."

Theo set his empty tray at the far end of the table. "Let's eat." He took a seat and Bradley took the one beside him.

Susan preceded him to the opposite side of the table and he pulled out the chair she put her hand on and pushed it in after she sat. He took the last seat which was probably Autumn's. He wondered where he'd be placed if there came a time when he'd have a meal with the whole family. He'd choose head of table, if only so he could see Susan's face better.

Each of the three served themselves from the nearest dish then passed them to the left. Gary loaded his plate as each item passed him.

Theo sipped his wine and studied Gary. Questions were going to begin. He'd rather Susan found out more about him privately, but mostly he didn't mind that the guys cared enough to protect her.

"Gary, did you grow up in town?"

"No. I came for college. They have a really great law enforcement program here."

Theo toyed with his fork. "You must have been on campus when Susan was."

Gary hoped Theo wasn't implying any impropriety. He'd checked Susan's background while working on the serial killer case when her husband had been a suspect. "All four years I was there. My first year was her last for her bachelors. Then she moved into the law building. Despite some of my justice classes also being in there, I never ran into her."

"Really?" Susan said. "I didn't know we went to the same school."

Theo narrowed his eyes. "How do you know all that?"

Gary shrugged. "I'm a detective." He might as well lay it all out there. "I also know you were only a few months out of college when you took over the reins of AAJ Electronics. Your father would be proud of how well you've done with the company."

Theo tipped his head down. "Thanks. I was in the office with Dad every chance I got." He gazed at Gary. "Once I finished high school, he made sure to schedule planning meetings for when I could be present. I knew how to run the company by the time I had to take over."

"Good for you. A lot of jobs would have been lost if you'd floundered."

Gary wasn't trying to stroke Theo's ego, just stating his thoughts. If it helped get the guys' approval to date Susan, all the better.

Bradley cleared his throat. "Why police work?"

"When I was a kid, I wanted to be a fireman." He grinned. "Probably most boys do. But in my teens I decided I didn't want to run into burning buildings. I still wanted to help the public, so becoming a policeman seemed the next best option."

"It's still dangerous. You could get shot," Susan said.

Gary cut a tender piece of meat. "That's why I got my degree. So I could earn my detectives badge quicker. There's still risk, but not as much as the cop on the street." He popped the succulent morsel into his mouth, enjoying the blend of flavors. He wished he could enjoy such tasty meals on a regular basis. He either picked up take-out on his way home or threw together something he'd only call edible. Although he was a pretty good cook when he had the time to enjoy it.

Conversation became less personal and more relaxed. An hour after they'd finished eating, Gary pushed back his chair. "I've enjoyed this evening, but I'm getting an early start in the morning, so I better leave."

Susan stood. "Start? You're going somewhere?"

"I'm visiting my sister, Melanie, for the weekend. My niece is in a dance performance."

"That's sweet of you. How old is she?"

"Angie is seven. She's in ballet and...something else." She'd been in ballet since she was four, but the other type of dance was new this year.

Susan took his hand and led him to the front door. It was the first time they'd held hands that didn't involve comforting her after a scare. He liked her warm, soft skin and imagined her hands sliding up his bare chest to the back of his neck.

At the door, she faced him but didn't let go of his hand. "Thanks for putting up with Theo and Bradley. I wasn't sure what to expect from them."

"I like them. Thanks for inviting me. Do you think I passed?"

Her cheeks turned pink. "I think so." She kissed his cheek. "Give me a call when you get back?"

"Most definitely." He kissed her forehead. Maybe next time he'd get to her mouth. "Have fun in the postmortem." He grinned when she bit her lip. He let himself out and whistled on his way to the car. That had gone better than he expected.

~~~

The guys had cleared the table and sat in the living room. She dropped down at the opposite end of the couch from Bradley and turned so she faced both men. Tonight, they would give their opinions. And Susan would listen this time, unlike when they'd shared their thoughts on Brian.

 She pulled a leg up and wrapped her hands around it. "What did you think?"

Theo leaned forward, and steepled his fingers. "He knew we were checking him out."

Susan gave a nervous chuckle. "Well, of course. We haven't gone out yet, and I asked him to join us for dinner. Only an idiot wouldn't have figured that out. And I wouldn't date an idiot."

Bradley rested his ankle on his other knee. "He sounded honest and cares about you. He wasn't falsely cheerful like…" He glanced at her and away.

None of them had totally dealt with Brian. Both had said they should have pushed harder with their opinions. And she regretted giving in to her loneliness.

Susan laughed. "You can't accuse him of being too cheerful."

"I liked him," Theo said.

Bradley tossed a pillow at him. "That's because he said you're doing a good job at AAJ."

"No, it's not. It's because he said he wanted to be a fireman."

52

Bradley burst out laughing and a moment later, Theo joined him.

"Seriously, guys?"

Theo raised a hand. "No. We're not laughing at his original career choice. He's a softy under that tough cop exterior."

Bradley patted Susan's hand. "Before dinner, I told him I'd beat him up if he hurt you."

"Bradley!"

"It's fine. He said he'd deserve it and he wouldn't press charges."

She raised her eyebrows. Gary really was a nice guy. She believed he wouldn't intentionally hurt her. Now she was willing to find out if they were compatible, and maybe more.

Chapter 5

Gary checked his list then shifted his car into gear. He'd talked to employees at nine of the bars on his second list and struck out at all of them. Now onto number ten, Bar to Nowhere.

After a short drive, he turned into a half full parking lot. Not bad for four o'clock. It would be jumping after dinner. He parked near the door and entered the building. A long bar ran along the back wall, three large TVs aired sporting events turned low, booths lined two walls, tables with four chairs each filled the center, and in the corner, sat two pool tables.

After a server delivered drinks to a table, he approached her and displayed his badge. "Can I ask you some questions?"

She glanced at it. "Sure. Let's talk over there." She pointed to a hallway at the end of the bar, and headed that way, then turned to face him. "What do you want to know?"

Gary pulled out his phone, found the picture, and showed it to her. "Do you recognize this man as a customer?"

She stared at the picture, eyes narrowed, then they widened. "That's the serial killer."

"Yes. Has he been in here?"

She nodded. "Twice when I've been working. I remember because after I saw his picture on the news, I said to myself, 'Holy crap, that guy's been in the bar.'"

It took him by surprise. He'd shown the picture in nearly two dozen bars. Many of the people he'd questioned had recognized the picture, but none had seen him in person. Maybe he'd finally get somewhere on this case. He pocketed his phone.

"Did he come in with anyone?"

"No. He was alone."

"Did he meet someone here?"

"No. He sat alone at the bar." She pointed. "At the far end."

He was glad the information had stuck in her mind. "Do you remember anything else about him?"

She shrugged. "When the bartender wasn't serving drinks, she talked to him."

"Is that normal for her? Does she normally go back and talk to particular customers?"

She played with the end of her braid. "Sure. She talked more to good looking guys."

Gary tipped his head toward the bar. "Is that her?" Maybe he'd get a chance to talk to someone who'd had direct contact with Jeffers.

She shook her head. "No. She doesn't work here anymore. Marcy took her place."

Shoot. The current bartender wouldn't have had contact.

"What's the old bartender's name?" He retrieved his phone, ready to take notes.

"California Jackson."

He paused. "Seriously?"

She shrugged. "Hey. I didn't name her."

A thought struck him. "What color is her hair?"

"Dark blonde. But it was colored. Sometimes I saw dark roots."

He waved a hand, taking in the room. "Would anyone else have seen him? Another bartender or server?"

"I don't know. Derek's the other bartender. Maybe he knows something. He'll be working tomorrow. Marie, the other waitress that has my timeslot, will be in then, too."

"By the way, can I get your name?"

"Janice Hastings."

He produced a card. "Thank you, Janice. You've been really helpful. If you think of anything else about him, can you give me a call?"

She took the card and slipped it into a pocket. "Sure thing."

"Is the owner here?" Maybe he could get California's address.

"No. That would be Derek."

A lead. Now, if he could find this California Jackson and see what Jeffers had told her. Maybe he'd find out if Jeffers had dated anyone.

~~~

Susan had gotten in the habit of peering at her porch as she turned into the driveway. It'd been a couple of weeks since the last stalker gift, but today there was another present. Her heart stuttered and she hit the brakes, then rolled down her window and pointed. Gary, reassuringly following behind, would know what she meant.

Susan pushed the garage door button and drove in. She and her daughter gathered their possessions. "Autumn, here's the door key." She held it out. "Go on inside, and don't forget to hit the security button like I showed you. I need to talk to Detective Wassman."

Gary had pulled into the driveway behind her car.

"Mom."

Susan squatted so she was eye level with Autumn. "Please, honey. Set the table and I'll be in shortly."

Autumn sighed, then dropped her shoulders. "Yes, Mom."

"Thank you, honey." Susan stayed beside the car until the back door closed, then joined Gary outside.

Halfway to the porch, he turned. She didn't know if he'd heard or sensed her.

He walked back to her. "Are you sure you want to see this?" He must have been close enough to tell what it was.

"It's not a dead animal, is it?"

"Not this time."

She wished all the scary messages and whatever they meant would go away, but since they wouldn't, she'd deal with it. She drew in a long breath. "Then I should see it."

He rested a warm hand on the back of her waist and walked beside her. She stopped at the bottom step.

A doll, wearing a black and red plaid dress, lay on the porch with a steak knife sticking out of its chest. It was a copy-cat eighteen inch doll like the American Girl dolls Autumn owned. Its hair was brown, like Autumn's. Under it was a piece of paper with black writing, like all the others.

Gary dropped his hand from her back and took his warmth with it. Cold. That's how this made her feel. She'd hoped this was all a sick joke that the perpetrator had grown tired of.

She hugged her arms to her body. "Do you think th-that's supposed to represent Autumn?"

"I don't know." He climbed to the step below the porch deck, and squatted, then set a large bag and gloves beside it.

He snapped some photos, gloved his hands and bagged the doll and knife separately.

She would have thought getting the doll out of her sight would make her feel better. No such luck. Now her gaze focused on the wide black letters on the page. Half behind Gary, she couldn't see enough of the message to read it.

He took a couple of pictures as she stepped up beside him. All the letters became hateful words.

He didn't
kill your
Daughter

Susan gasped. She never considered that Autumn might have been in danger from Brian. He'd been arrested before she'd found out he was the killer the police had been looking for, and he'd only killed women. "Do you think that means Brian tried to kill Autumn but didn't succeed?"

"If it weren't for the note about the flowers, I might think the parent of one of Jeffers' victims had written this one. Angry that your child lived but not theirs." Gary slipped the sheet into a third bag, stood, stripped the gloves off then took her hand.

"While you were with Brian, did Autumn have any accidents or near accidents? Did she have any unexplained illnesses?"

She narrowed her eyes and stared into the distance. "No accidents. No near accidents as far as I know. And the rare times she was sick, it was mild."

He took her hand, leading her to believe she wouldn't like the question.

"What happens to her inheritance if she dies?"

"She inherited a third of Anthony's holdings. It would be divided equally between Theo, Bradley, and me."

"So if Brian had killed Autumn, then you afterward, without anyone realizing it was murder, he would have owned about one-ninth of AAJ Electronics and whatever other cash and property."

Her legs trembled and she placed her hand on Gary's chest so she wouldn't fall. Her daughter might have died because of her misjudgment.

The bagged doll bumped her thigh as Gary wrapped an arm around her waist. "Let's step down to the ground."

Once on secure footing, he set the bags down and wrapped his fingers around her arms. His warmth radiated up into her chest. She dragged in a breath and stared into his eyes.

"Susan. Don't go there. What this message tells me is that Brian knew he could inherit indirectly. For whatever reason, he chose not to kill Autumn"—he pointed at the bags beside their feet—"and that person wasn't happy with his choice."

She sagged against him and his arms came around her,

warming her more. "Despite how they snipped at each other, Brian couldn't hurt her." There'd been some good in him after all. Not enough to save the women he'd killed, but enough to keep her daughter alive.

The other garage door rising drew her attention. Theo drove into the garage, and moments later, he and Bradley joined them in front of the house.

Gary dropped his arms from around her.

Theo playfully punched Gary's arm. "Hey, what's with hugging in the front yard?"

His face reddened. "I—"

"He was offering support. Another note came."

"What?" Bradley picked up the plastic encased paper. "Oh, wow."

Theo wrapped an arm around her shoulders. She glanced up at his face. He gazed at Gary with a severe expression.

"Do you think," Theo said, "this person wants to rectify the mistake?"

She gasped and Theo pulled her tighter to his side.

Gary shrugged. "I wouldn't rule it out."

Theo straightened his shoulders. "We're getting Autumn a bodyguard until this is over."

It seemed like everything was spinning out of control. "Do you think that's necessary? She doesn't go out on her own."

Theo's face was grim. "Since I don't know, we can't chance it."

"You're right." Why did she question it when the most important thing was Autumn's safety?

Theo glanced at Gary, as if for approval. "I want someone inside with her at school and the after school program."

Gary took out his phone. "If you don't know who to call, I can offer a couple of suggestions. People I trust."

"Thanks," Theo said. "We've never had the need."

"Give me your number and I'll send you their contact info and websites. They have background on all their employees."

Theo gave his number and a few moments later, it dinged with a received message.

Gary squeezed Theo's shoulder. "Glad you got those cameras in place. I'm calling the security company to have them send me the video for this afternoon. Hopefully, there's something more revealing on it than last time."

The front door opened, and Susan turned to it.

Autumn stood in the doorway, her gaze darting between the adults. "Mom?"

Susan rushed up the steps and wrapped her daughter in her arms. All the talk about keeping Autumn safe, and she'd forgotten Autumn was alone inside the house. "Your brothers came home while I was talking to Detective Wassman. Let's go inside and get dinner on the table."

She glanced over her shoulder at Gary. "Thank you." From the first, Susan had thought she was the only target of this stalker. It scared her ten times worse to find out her daughter might also be in danger.

~~~

Gary arrived at Bar to Nowhere ten minutes after it opened. He hoped to catch the owner before he had too many customers. He entered, and two women, sitting at a table, looked at him then turned away.

He made his way to the bar where a man loaded stemmed glasses into an overhead rack, his back to the room. That wouldn't prevent the man from seeing Gary with the mirror in front of him. It didn't seem like too many people would order wine in this place. Not that it was a roughneck bar, more blue collar.

Gary pulled out his badge. "Derek?"

The man spun around. "Who wants to know?"

Gary flipped his badge open. "Me. Detective Gary Wassman."

The man leaned over the bar and narrowed his eyes at the identification, then studied Gary's face. Most people didn't pay that much attention. He leaned his elbows on the bar top. "What can I do for you, detective?"

Gary returned his badge to his pocket and pulled out his phone. He showed it to Derek. "Do you remember this man as a customer?"

Derek took the phone from Gary and stared at it as long as he'd studied Gary's badge. "Isn't this that serial killer from a few months back?"

"Yeah. Did you ever see him in here?"

He handed the phone back. "I don't think so, but if he'd only been in a couple of times, I wouldn't have noticed him. I tend to notice the ladies more than the men." He grinned.

"I hear that California Jackson served him his drinks."

"She doesn't work here anymore."

Gary shifted his feet. "Did she leave on her own or was she fired?"

"It was her decision. Gave a week's notice. Better than some."

"When?"

Derek shrugged a shoulder. "I don't remember. It'd be in my records."

"Can we check? And I'd like to get her address."

Derek took a step then turned back. "Why do you want to know?"

"I'm hoping she can shed light on a case I'm working on."

The man raised a brow. He continued to the end of the bar, and lifted the countertop gate. "This way."

Gary followed him to a small office past the restrooms.

Derek opened a filing cabinet, rifled through some folders, and pulled out a single piece of paper. He handed it to Gary. "Here. Take what you need from this." He crossed his arms as Gary looked over the information. "She was liked by the customers, so she didn't quit because of that. I think she moved on."

Gary hoped not. Her last day was about a month after Jeffers' death. Her address was a few blocks from the bar, so she could have walked. Maybe she didn't have a car. Not that she would have wanted to walk home that late at night.

Gary figure a bar owner would need proof of age for serving alcohol. "Do you have a driver's license number or state ID for her?"

Derek leaned flipped to the next page. "I need one or the other as proof of age."

Gary noted all the information for a license number, hoping it would get him a current address if this one was wrong. "Thanks. You've been very helpful."

He drove to the address and knocked on the door. A short, natural blonde opened the door. Somehow not what he was expecting. "California Jackson?"

"No. She moved. I've been here a couple of months, but I still get junk mail with her name on it."

"Thanks for your time." He got back in his car. One chance left at finding her, but not everybody updated the address on their license when they moved. And how much could a bartender tell him about a couple of conversations she had months ago?

Chapter 6

Susan didn't call him every night, and he didn't know which nights she would call, but Gary waited with anticipation each evening as soon as the clock hit nine, after Autumn had gone to bed. He either read a book or watched TV to tamp down his anticipation.

As if on cue, his cell phone rang. Gary flipped the footrest up and leaned back. "Hi, honey." He hadn't used an endearment before, and wasn't sure how she'd react. Maybe the first time he said it should have been in person.

Her breath hitched. "Hi, Gary."

"Autumn get to sleep all right?"

"Yes. We're reading *Harry Potter* at bedtime, and she had me read past a scary part before we stopped."

"Which book?"

"Book two. *The Chamber of Secrets.* Have you read them?"

"Guilty." He chuckled. "Don't look for them on my bookshelf. I keep them in a closet."

"Lots of adults have read them. I'm enjoying them along with Autumn." She lowered her voice. "Don't tell anyone, but when one of Autumn's brothers reads to her, I have to go back and read what I missed."

"I can lend you mine if you want. Then you won't have to sneak Autumn's copy."

She laughed. "No. That's fine."

He loved her laughter. He'd only heard it once before,

when he'd been to dinner.

Gary hated to spoil her good mood, but he needed to make sure Autumn would be safe. "Sorry to bring this up, but did Theo line up a bodyguard for Autumn?"

"Yes." Her breath rasped out. "He starts first thing tomorrow. He came to the house yesterday to go over everything with us and for Autumn to become familiar with him."

"Who is it? I'd like to call and give him details about the case."

"Chris Billings."

"He's excellent. He's got kids of his own, so he's comfortable with them."

"Autumn took to him right away. Especially after he showed her pictures of his children."

"That's good." Gary was relieved she would be in capable hands. "Assuming I passed the test at dinner, I'd like to take you out."

She snickered. "You know you passed. Fortunately, I have in-house sitters."

"How about dinner Wednesday? I can follow you home as usual, and we'll leave after you change."

"I'll need to change?"

He closed his eyes, imagining what he'd want to see her in. Short skirt, low neckline. "Do you want to go someplace casual like Jackie Rae's or a nicer place like Cecile's Turf Loft?"

"You'd be willing to go to Cecile's?"

He grinned. "Hey, don't sound surprised. I've eaten there." Once. It was a disaster of a date, but he thought it would be a nice date place with the right woman. "Or something else of your choice." He was flexible, but he wanted her to know he would be willing to go to an expensive restaurant, if that was what she preferred.

"Do you like to dance?"

To have Susan in his arms, even if it was only to dance would be half of his dream. "Yes. It's been a while, but I enjoy it. I pretty much only dance at weddings." Before his junior prom he'd begged his mother to let him take dance lessons since the girl he'd had a crush on had said yes. He didn't want to be one of the guys who put his arms around his girl and shuffled back and forth.

"How about Grilled Delight?"

"I haven't been there, but I heard it's good." A jacket and no tie should fit in. "Okay. On Wednesday, I'll follow you home and wait for you. I'm looking forward to it."

"Me, too. Have a nice night, Gary."

"I enjoyed talking to you. Good night, Susan."

He dropped his phone on his chest. He hoped he wouldn't embarrass himself trying to rush through dinner so they could get to the part where he got to hold her.

~~~

Susan pulled into the garage and Gary parked behind her in the driveway.

Autumn would be home any minute with Chris Billings. The first two days had gone fine. Chris had picked up Autumn in the morning and driven to school. He entered her class-rooms with her to check them out, then sat in a chair in the hallway across from her room. They'd discussed him bringing her directly home after school, but they decided to have her continue the after school program to keep Autumn's life as normal as possible.

Susan got out of her car and waited for Gary. "Come on inside." She gave an appreciative once-over of his charcoal suit and open-collared white shirt. His blond hair was just long enough to curl on the ends. Every time she'd seen him, he'd worn a suit. This one was better quality. It fit his muscular shoulders better, but was cut for his narrower abs. It must have been tailored while his others were off the rack. He'd worn a dress-up suit for her, and she appreciated the extra care he took.

In the kitchen, she pointed at a chair. "You can make yourself at home while I change. Do you want some water?" She hoped the delicious aroma of Miriam's lasagna didn't make him wish they'd stayed here for dinner.

"I'm fine."

She agreed with that. "Autumn and Chris should be here shortly. Then we'll have to wait until Theo and Bradley get home."

Susan ran up to her room. The night before, as soon as they'd said goodnight, she'd picked out what to wear for dinner. She stripped out of her suit, freshened up and put on the dress. After renewing her makeup, she pulled the pins from her hair, and brushed it out. A spin in front of the full length mirror showed she looked perfect. The fine sapphire fabric displayed her curves and would flair when they danced. Then she transferred essentials from her purse to a small wristlet that she could dance with.

Voices grew louder as she approached the stairs, and she paused at the top.

Autumn's excited voice floated upstairs. "Mr. Billings was my show-and-tell in class his first day. The other kids made him tell them a story about how he saved someone."

Gary chuckled. "I've done career day at a few schools. Kids ask some pretty strange questions."

She heard the door to the garage open, and Autumn's happy squeal. "Bradley. Theo." Susan knew her daughter would give each brother a hug.

She couldn't help smiling at Bradley's stage whisper. "Hey, kiddo, you ready for the no-mom party?"

Autumn giggled. "Yes."

Susan descended the stairs and entered the kitchen to find Theo with an arm over Autumn's shoulder.

Gary noticed her first, and his eyes lit up. Her heart fluttered. She joined the group, and stopped beside Gary.

Gary and Chris shook hands. "Since you're all here, I'll leave," the bodyguard said. He squatted so he was eye to eye with Autumn. "I'll see you tomorrow morning."

"Bye, Mr. Billings."

He straightened and nodded. "Nice seeing you all." He left through the door to the garage.

Susan hugged her daughter already having told Autumn she was going to dinner with Gary. "You be good for your brothers. I won't be home until after you're in bed, so I'll see you in the morning."

Autumn glanced over her shoulder at Gary. If things worked out with him, Susan would have to organize some activities for the three of them to do together.

She reached for Gary without thinking about it, but somehow, it seemed right. "You ready?"

He smiled and took her hand. A quick glance at Bradley and Theo showed that they'd noticed. She didn't understand it, but she and Gary seemed to share a connection.

She led the way through the garage, and he opened the passenger door of his car for her then he took the driver's seat.

"Is this your personal car?" It didn't have the small antenna for a police band radio that the other car had.

"Yes. I know it's not flashy or expensive."

He shouldn't unfavorably compare himself to Susan and her household, as if money was the most important criteria. She leaned back in the seat. "Wow, this is really nice. Anthony bought me my first couple Lexus. I stayed with the same brand, although I chose a cheaper model."

He backed out of the driveway. "I called Grilled Delight to make reservations, but they don't take them."

She laughed. "At least it's Wednesday. Don't even try to get in on a Friday or Saturday unless you're there before five."

"You've been there before?"

"Yes, but it's been a while."

Gary parked a few spaces from the door and escorted her

inside. They stopped in front of the hostess' desk. Susan didn't recognize the young woman.

"Two for dinner," Gary said.

The woman marked off a table on her sheet and picked up two menus. "All right. This…" Her eyes widened. "Is that you, Aunt Susan?"

Susan studied the woman. "Oh, wow. Megan, I can't believe it's you. You're so grown up. You must have been about fourteen when I last saw you."

They hugged, and Megan stepped back with a grin. "I'll show you to your table. Mom and Dad are going to be thrilled when I tell them you're here."

After they were seated, Megan rushed off. Susan leaned forward. "I'm sorry. I somehow thought we'd be anonymous, but I didn't expect Megan to be here."

"Hey, no problem. Aunt Susan, huh?"

"Yes. Anthony and Bill were childhood friends."

"I think it's great that you'll see old friends." He didn't look upset about it. Brian would have, but she shouldn't even be thinking about him.

Before she had a chance to open her menu, Bill and Wendy marched up to the table. Wendy dragged Susan out of her seat and hugged her. "Susan, it's so good to see you. I've worried about you."

"It's great to see you, too."

Bill gave Susan a hug as Gary stood, then the men shook hands. "Gary Wasmann."

"Bill Forsythe." The man didn't immediately release Gary's hand, but studied her date. Gary didn't flinch. Bill put an arm around Susan's shoulders and spoke to Gary. "You treat our Susan right."

Gary glanced at Susan. "That's my plan. She's a wonderful woman."

"What do you do?"

"Bill!" Wendy said.

"I'm a police detective."

Bill gripped Gary's shoulder. "A good solid job. Well, you two enjoy your dinner. I'm sending out a bottle of wine on the house."

"That's very nice of you. Thank you," Gary said.

Susan was grateful Gary took the gift graciously. She was afraid his pride would make him refuse and cause some tension.

Bill clasped Susan's hand. "And you. Don't be a stranger. We've missed you."

She dipped her head. "I'm sorry. It's been hard." She would have burst into tears seeing them soon after Anthony died. In her grief stricken world, it had been emotionally easier not to attempt it. The couple headed back to the kitchen.

They resumed their seats, and Gary grinned. "I hadn't expected anything like that."

"I didn't really either. I sort of thought they wouldn't notice me. It surprised me that Megan was hostessing. I still imagine her as a little girl." She wrapped her fingers around Gary's hand. "You didn't mind, did you?"

"Not at all. I think it's nice meeting people who care so much for you."

"Thank you." She blew out a breath. "Okay, let's figure out what we want to eat. Everything is good."

On the phone, they'd found lots to talk about, but face-to-face might become awkward. She shouldn't have feared. Gary kept the conversation rolling and any silences were comfortable.

Dessert was ordered after the meal, and Susan swirled her fork into the last of the chocolate frosting. Gary turned her hand to redirect the fork into his mouth. Her breath stopped. His blue gaze stayed on her face as the chocolate goodness disappeared into his mouth and he slowly withdrew the fork. That shouldn't be so sexy. But combined with the warmth of his hand over her wrist, she was ready to go where the chocolate did. Too bad he didn't leave any chocolate on his lips she could kiss off.

"Mmm. I wanted to see if your dessert tasted as good as my cherry pie."

"And does it?" She almost didn't recognize her breathy voice.

He grinned. "No, but…" He turned her hand and kissed her fingers. "You do."

Susan never thought she'd feel melty, gooey inside again. "Ready to dance?"

"I've been waiting all evening for this." Gary paid the check with cash. He stood and held out his hand. "Shall we?"

Her heart fluttered. More than ready. She placed her hand in his and followed him to the bar. A door separated the bar and dance floor from the dining room. Music played quietly until the door between opened, and the volume increased. Not that it was an obnoxious level in the bar.

She'd had only one evening of dancing since all those wonderful times with Anthony, and that had been the day she married Brian. He'd danced as little as he could get away with. Looking back, she wondered if it was because he didn't want to hold her. She didn't want to think about him again. Ever.

Gary stopped and took her other hand, his eyes full of concern. "Hey, are you all right?"

She must have given herself away. "Just thinking about things I don't want to think about."

"Do you want to—"

She placed her fingers over his mouth. "No. I want to dance. I've been looking forward to this since we made the date."

Her forwardness amazed her, much more than when she'd dated Anthony. She'd been an inexperienced college student, and he'd been mature and sexy. Again, not something she should be thinking about.

Gary led her a few steps onto the dance floor. It was the space between songs, and they wouldn't know what type of song would be next. Her small wristlet dangled from her right hand, and she switched it to her left.

"Do you want me to put that in my jacket pocket?"

Then she wouldn't have to worry about bumping him with it. And, if she dared, she could get creative with her hands. She handed the purse over.

The music began with a slow number. Gary wrapped his arm around her waist and held her hand with his. His feet moved, and hers followed automatically. His hand grew warmer on her back, yet he kept a couple of inches between them. Maybe she shouldn't have suggested this for a first date. She had a feeling she'd feel the imprint of his hand long after he removed it.

Gary's cheek brushed the side of her head. "You used to dance here with Anthony?"

She tipped her head back to study him. "Yes. Does it bother you?"

He shook his head. "No. I think it's nice that you brought me to a place that you used to enjoy. I hope that I don't spoil your memories."

She laid her head on his shoulder, drawing them closer together. "Nothing can change the good memories I have, but I can't live in memories." She slid her hand into the hair at his nape, and he pulled her tighter for a moment.

She'd never thought of herself as bold, but the evening talks with Gary made it easy to grow comfortable with him. Then to touch him like this made her long for things she thought she'd never want again. He was understanding and way too serious, then he'd say something funny.

The song ended and soft chatter emerged before it was covered again by music. She could do this all night. They danced three more songs before a faster tempo drove them to the bar where they both ordered sodas. The bottle of wine had nearly been empty when they finished dinner, and she was glad that Gary had switched to a non-alcoholic drink with her.

He picked up their glasses. "Let's go sit over there." He nodded toward a table set diagonal to the wall. They took seats where both could watch the dancers, but he shifted his chair, and their knees touched, maybe he wanted to maintain contact.

She enjoyed dancing with Gary, being held in his arms. She couldn't help her mind wandering to what they'd feel like dancing naked together, and where that would lead them.

He gulped down half his drink. "That was nice. You're a good dancer."

"Thanks. You're no slouch yourself. You didn't once step on my toes."

He took her hand, chilled from her glass and rubbed his warm fingers over her skin. "What kinds of things do you like to do?"

"I used to golf, but…" She couldn't show her face at the country club again after her husband, their star golf pro, had turned out to be a killer. She could have switched clubs, but she didn't have the heart for golf any longer.

Gary's hand closed down on hers. "I can see why you wouldn't want to do that anymore."

She stared into his eyes, at the obvious concern. "I could drive forty-five minutes to the next course over, but it's not worth it. I took up golf for Anthony. I enjoyed it, but—" She shrugged. "I don't miss it as much as I thought I might."

He resumed the gentle rubbing of her hand, and tingles shot up her arm. "What else do you like doing?"

"I like boating and swimming. At least I can still swim in the pool at home."

"Boating is out?"

Her gaze dropped to their hands. "Theo sold the lake house." She couldn't suppress the shiver.

His hands tightened again. "I'm sorry."

She hadn't been back inside after learning Brian had killed those women in its basement. Except for a few prized mementos and kitchenware, the house had been sold with its contents.

The bed used in committing the heinous crimes was disposed of. No one wanted those nightmares.

"Theo's closing on another house on the other side of the lake in a couple of weeks. Then he can move the boat, canoes, and kayaks from behind our home."

"I bet he took a big loss on that."

"There wasn't a mortgage on it, but he had to sell way below market value. Theo considered tearing it down and rebuilding, but that would have cost more." Susan sighed and shook her head. "You know, the realtor said that if we wanted to wait a bit, he could get more than market value by advertising in certain places. Maybe even score a bidding war. He said some people want to own a home where multiple murders occurred."

No surprise registered on his face. "There are some really sick people out there."

"Yes. I couldn't imagine someone like that living across the street from Meredith Somers." Theo had been as repulsed as she'd been when the realtor brought it up. "After the boat's back in the water, do you want to go boating or kayaking?"

"That sounds fun. Let me know when. Do you want to dance again?"

The evening flew by, and Susan couldn't believe midnight approached. She yawned.

Gary leaned back. "I thought you were sagging there. I'm keeping you out too late. Let me take you home."

She nodded. "I've got a deposition tomorrow. I should have called it quits earlier, but I really enjoyed tonight."

He walked beside her with his arm around her waist. At the passenger door, he handed over her purse. "Here. So I don't forget later."

"Thanks for keeping it for me."

A short, nearly silent drive brought them to her house. He was probably as tired as she was.

In the driveway, Gary rounded the front of the car and opened her door. He held out his hand and helped her out, a great excuse for them to touch. Small lights illuminated the walkway to the front steps. He walked with his hand on the small of her back.

Susan felt jittery inside, probably a combination of worry at how she'd react if he kissed her and worry at how she'd feel if he didn't. Did she want him to? Yes. If he didn't, should she kiss him?

As they reached the bottom step, the porch light came on, and he glanced up at it.

She knew what he was thinking. "It's a motion detector light."

He chuckled. "Good. I thought someone was going to intrude on our goodnight kiss."

They stepped up to the door, and Gary pulled her into his arms. "I'm glad you suggested we go to Grilled Delight. I had a really good time tonight."

"I did, too."

"I enjoyed the conversation, but I really enjoyed holding, um, dancing with you."

She giggled and blamed it on the wine. "I enjoyed holding you, too." She slid her hands up his chest and around his neck. He'd already said he was going to kiss her, but she didn't know what to expect.

His lips touched hers, light and way too brief. He pulled back, and stared into her eyes. She hoped he didn't see the disappointment.

His fingers threaded through her hair, his thumbs on her cheeks. He leaned in slow, pausing a moment before his lips claimed hers. Maybe it was a testing of the waters the first time because there was nothing hesitant about this kiss. The tip of his tongue tickled her lip, and she opened for him. His hand slipped from her hair down to the small of her back, and he pulled her closer.

Dancing had been hours of foreplay leading to this moment. Her body craved sensations she'd nearly forgotten, and he delivered exactly what she needed. If her life was different, she'd invite him in, but too much stood in the way.

Though reluctant to pull back, Susan rested her forehead on his chest. His rapid heartbeat under her ear letting her know he'd been as affected as she had.

Gary ran his fingers through her hair. "I'm sorry. I'm rushing you."

"No." She gave him a quick kiss, his concern making her want him even more. "It was perfect. You're the first man I've been interested in since…" She flicked her gaze to the door then back to him. "I'm being bombarded with all these crazy mixed emotions, but I don't regret anything about tonight." A small smile escaped. "And especially not that kiss."

He grinned. "Good. Because I've got a lot more of those to give you." He gave her another, just a short one. "Pleasant dreams, Susan."

Probably erotic dreams. She dug into her wristlet for her house key, shoved it into the lock and opened the door. Before she could step inside, Gary pulled her back and gave her a searing kiss.

"Goodnight." He nudged her through the door and pulled it closed between them.

She flipped the lock and leaned against the door. Their date was better than she'd ever imagined.

The creak of a floorboard made her heart race, and a voice in the dark came to her. "How was your evening?"

She clutched a hand to her chest. "Theo! You scared me."

He stepped from the dark living room into the lighted foyer. "Sorry. I was waiting up for you and fell asleep." He rubbed a hand over his face. Theo preferred watching movies with the lights off. "What time is it?"

"Twelve-fifteen. And it was a really nice evening. We went to Grilled Delight, and danced after dinner."

"Wow. You never went there with—Sorry."

"With Brian. The place never seemed right for him. Or

maybe he never seemed right for the place. I think Bill and Wendy liked Gary."

"Of course they did." Theo had accepted Gary so quickly. He gave her a one armed hug. "I'm glad you had a good evening. See you in the morning."

She grinned. "Thanks for waiting up, Dad."

Without Theo and Bradley, she didn't know how she could have survived losing Anthony or the fiasco with Brian. Now she needed her stalker gone so she could have a chance with Gary.

Chapter 7

Gary leaned back in his office chair, remembering the evening before. Despite Susan telling him there was dancing, he hadn't expected to have her in his arms for more than a couple of songs. Once she was in his embrace, it was hard to let her go.

For Susan to be able to make life-altering decisions about them, he had to solve this stalker case. More important, she and her daughter needed to be safe.

He flipped the stalker folder open, and rubbed the back of his neck. In his caseload, Susan's case wasn't a top priority. In his heart, hers was the only one that mattered.

Gary hadn't succeeded in finding any information on California Jackson. Her license number ended up belonging to a man. Maybe the bar owner had written it down incorrectly, or she had a fake ID. He'd hoped she might have taken a job at another bar, but hadn't come across her.

His boss walked past with a coffee in his hand.

"Hey, Luke. I have a question."

Luke made a quick turn and sat on the edge of Gary's desk. "What's up?"

"This Argyle stalker is driving me crazy. I don't have anything on her. I thought I'd gotten a lead with a bartender Jeffers talked to, but she's disappeared."

"What happened?"

Gary dug a paper out of his file. "California Jackson used

to bartend at Bar to Nowhere that Jeffers went to at least twice. According to a waitress, he sat at the bar and talked to California. I figured he might have told her something useful, but she moved from the address the bar owner provided, and the driver's license she used was incorrect. I'm at a dead end."

"It sounds like California Jackson might have been an alias. But it's worth trying the USPS National Change of Address site."

Gary palmed his forehead. "I totally forgot about that. I'll give it a try. Thanks."

Luke fanned out the remaining folders on the desk, and lifted one. "How's the Cramer case coming?"

Of course, Luke would pick the case Gary had spent the least time on. "I'm waiting on some information, but there are a couple of things I could follow up on today."

His boss's lips pressed together. He dropped the folder, and stood. "Get on it." He disappeared into his office.

Gary accessed the change of address site with the special law enforcement option and entered California's name and last known address. No forwarding address had been filed. He'd hoped, for Susan's sake, the name wasn't an alias. There were too many dead ends.

While he was on the website, he might as well try to find Jeffers' sister. He typed in Callista Jeffers, then flipped open his Argyle file to get her mother's address. Once that was typed in, the results showed an address updated four years before. It looked familiar. He tapped a finger on his desk, filtering the address through his memory. Maybe in the Brian Jeffers file.

Gary dug out his folder on the serial killer case from the filing cabinet behind his desk and scanned each page. There! On the page of notes of the previous golf clubs where Jeffers worked was this same address. Jeffers and his sister had lived together when Jeffers was pursuing a woman at another club he'd worked.

It seemed that if Jeffers had moved from that address, his

sister probably did, too. But it was worth checking into.

Gary looked at his watch. The round-trip should take less than five hours. If he left now, he might have time to do a little work on the Cramer case when he returned.

It took two hours and fifteen minutes to reach his destination. He slowed once he reached the street, studying the neighborhood. Nothing like where Jeffers had lived with Susan. This was lower-middle-class. A long line of townhouse-style apartments lined the street, two units per building. He pulled to the curb at 632, got out and climbed the steps.

The doorbell chimed pleasantly when he pushed it. After a minute, he rang it again. No car sat in the driveway. He crossed the porch and rang the bell of the adjoining apartment. Within moments, the door opened.

Gary flipped his badge open. "Detective Gary Wassman." The woman in the doorway glanced at it and back to his face.

He pointed at the apartment beside them. "Do you know who lives there?"

She frowned. "Joan and Alex Heath. Is there a problem?"

Missed again. "No. I'm looking for a previous tenant. Callista Jeffers."

She bit her lip. "She lived there before the Heaths. I think her brother lived with her."

"Do you remember if she moved out when he did?"

The woman leaned against the doorframe. "He left a month or two before her. She said he was finding them a new place."

"Did you talk to her much?" He needed something new.

She shrugged a shoulder. "We talked some. I didn't know she was leaving until one day there was a moving truck next door. Her brother had come back to help her move."

"Did they say where they were going?"

She shook her head. "No."

"Do you know the date they moved?"

The woman's eyebrows rose. "No. You could ask the landlord." She pointed further up the street. "He lives in the first house past all the townhouses."

"Thanks for your time." Gary drove to the house she pointed out.

A man answered Gary's knock. He showed his badge. "Detective Gary Wassman. I'm looking for information about one of your former tenants. Callista Jeffers."

"What do you want to know?"

"Can you tell me when she moved?"

The man leaned against the door frame. "Has something happened?"

"I'm hoping she can give me some information in an on-going case."

The landlord straightened up, and took a step back. "I'll have to check my records. Come on in."

Gary followed him through a living room, down a hallway, and into a home office. He stayed at the door as the man opened a cabinet and pulled out a file. The guy set the folder on top of the cabinet and flipped it open, then lifted the top sheet and rattled off a date. It fit in with when Jeffers had started work at Willow Ridge Golf Club.

"Did they leave a forwarding address for return of their security deposit?"

Anger crossed the man's face. "They didn't get their security deposit back. They left the place a mess."

So much for that. "Do you remember what Callista looked like?" He still hadn't found any pictures of her.

"Seemed like she changed her hair color every month. Eyes the same color as her brother's, brown. Looked a little like him, but didn't have that prominent chin."

Gary shook the man's hand. "Thanks for the help."

Due to heavier traffic, it took longer to get back to the station. Gary ended up getting only an hour of phone calls in on the Cramer case before it was time to leave to follow Susan home.

He worried that since it was Thursday, the stalker might have left her another threat.

~~~

Susan should have called Gary to ask him to come up to the house after following her home. She wanted to kiss him again. Of course, it had to be in the short time before Autumn arrived. She glanced once in the rearview mirror before hitting the garage door button and turning into the drive.

She got out of the car and smiled. Gary had pulled up behind her space. Maybe he had the same craving. He got out of the car, but didn't look her way as he started up the front walk.

No, no, no. She hadn't checked. Her gaze darted to the front porch and back to Gary. He must have seen something. She hoped it was just a delivery of something one of the guys had ordered, a box with a smile on it.

Susan followed him. He paused and glanced back. "You might not want to see."

She stiffened her shoulders. "I'm the target. I need to see." It took a moment before she could convince her feet to move. She stepped to Gary's side, and he took her hand, giving it a squeeze. Together they approached the porch and whatever lay in wait.

A rope. Two steps up, she got the whole effect. A rope tied into a noose perfectly circled the words on the paper.

Time's

up

A full body shiver racked her. Gary pulled her tightly into his arms. It helped. A little.

Time's up. *Time's up.* She knew what that meant. Whoever had been leaving these messages decided it was time to kill her. Was the noose a reminder of how Brian had died, or telling her that she'd die the same way?

If someone wanted to shoot her, there'd probably be no

way to prevent it. But if this person did intend for her to hang, then maybe she could fight. Unless they knocked her out first. This whole time, she had imagined safety with her stepsons following her to work and Gary following her home.

Gary kissed the side of her head. "I won't let anything happen to you."

"But we don't know who it is. It might even be someone I know.

His arms tightened around her. "It's not likely someone you know, at least not someone close. They couldn't have hidden that kind of anger from you."

Wheels on pavement caught their attention. It was Autumn arriving with Chris. Susan didn't want her daughter seeing another threat. "Let's meet them at the driveway."

"Good idea. Once you go in, I'll take care of this."

Autumn and Chris got out of the car, and joined Susan and Gary at the edge of the driveway. Susan wrapped an arm around her daughter. They'd have to do something fun tonight, a distraction for both of them.

She touched Chris's arm. "Thank you. I think Gary wants to talk to you."

She nudged her daughter, and they walked toward the open garage. Beside her car, she glanced over her shoulder. Gary leaned into his trunk, probably getting the evidence bags.

Susan patted Autumns shoulder. "Let's see what Mrs. Devins cooked for dinner."

"Mom, can Grace come over tomorrow for a sleepover?"

It might be an even better distraction for Autumn. She'd accepted a bodyguard readily enough, but having a friend over would help Autumn's life feel more normal. Between the security system and the guys being home, she didn't have qualms about any of their safety. "I'll talk to your brothers about it. If we all agree, I'll give her mom a call."

~~~

Gary settled into his recliner and flipped through TV channels, but his thoughts remained on Susan. She'd suffered through the trauma of being married to a serial killer. Now a stalker accused her of causing his death.

With this new threat, he'd told Chris, Theo, and Bradley to be extra vigilant. The stalker was bound to make a move soon, and he hoped she was crazy enough to make a mistake.

The night before, he'd waited until a little after Susan's usual call time, and when she hadn't reached out to him, he called her to check on how she was doing after the last threat. He was glad he did. She'd started out sounding nervous and seemed relaxed by the time they said goodnight.

He had spent so much time trying to find Jeffers' sister to get her to tell him about any girlfriends he might have had, that it only just crossed his mind that maybe his sister could be the stalker. They'd shared an apartment in the last town he'd lived. She might have followed him to his new place.

Obviously that meant they were close. It did seem strange that he wouldn't have introduced his sister to Susan—maybe because he considered Susan his moneybags and nothing more.

His phone rang and he grinned. Susan's calls were the best part of his evening, and he was disappointed when she didn't call. "Hello, gorgeous."

He wished he could see how she reacted to that. After holding her for those hours while they danced, he felt she was comfortable with him saying something more personal.

She audibly drew in a breath. "Hi, Gary."

"Mom." Gary was surprised to hear Autumn since she was always in bed when he talked to Susan.

"Hold on, Gary."

He waited while Susan took care of her daughter.

"Sorry about that. Autumn's not happy because we wouldn't let her have a friend stay over."

"No problem. Autumn comes first. How about if the three of us do something then?" He hadn't intended to ask. It just popped out of his mouth, but it sounded like a great idea to him.

"Okay. I planned on taking Autumn to the street fair at City Park. Do you want to join us?"

"That sounds fun. We can get lunch there." He could be a bodyguard for them both. He hoped she hadn't planned on going alone.

"All right. Bradley will be relieved he doesn't have to go."

He was glad she'd planned on staying safe. "Great. I'll pick the two of you up at twelve."

He shifted, not comfortable with the question he needed to ask. "I have a case related question that I hate to ask. Do you know where Brian lived before you two married?"

Almost four years ago, in a group of memories no doubt she'd rather forget. The long silence started to get uncomfortable. "I can't give you the address, but I think I can get there. We stopped by once when Brian needed to pick something up, but he didn't invite me in. We did some weekends away when we wanted to be alone."

He tapped his fingers on the armrest. "Didn't that seem strange that he didn't have you come inside?"

"I thought he was uncomfortable with the wealth of this house."

"I don't mind having you over to my house, even if I only have six rooms and no pool." He would love to have Susan at his house overnight. Maybe the next time Autumn went to her friend's house for a sleepover. At least for dinner, if she wasn't ready for more.

Susan huffed. "I grew up in a four room house. I know what it is to scrimp and save and not always get what you want because your parents couldn't afford it. Sometimes, I think Autumn has it too easy, and she'll end up spoiled."

It was nice to hear of her humble beginnings. She'd been through four years of college and about to start law school when she met her first husband, and he was sure, even without his financial support, she would have finished. "I know you'll make sure that doesn't happen. Theo and Bradley grew up with wealth, and they don't seem to be spoiled brats."

"Sorry. I hear Autumn. I've got to go."

"All right. I'll see you tomorrow. Goodnight."

Gary set his phone on the table beside him. The Jeffers' sister angle didn't seem quite right. His sister wouldn't complain about not getting flowers. Brothers didn't give their sisters flowers, at least none he knew. He was likely back to asking Callista about girlfriends. If he ever found her.

Chapter 8

Susan, Gary and Autumn had enjoyed lunch from various food trucks. They worked their way through half the craft stalls, Autumn in the lead. She probably wasn't supposed to notice, but Gary kept alert, scanning the crowd.

The first vendor to grab Susan's attention was a stall with hundreds of silk scarves of every color and design. She stopped and contemplated a scarf a local artist had created. She might never wear it, but it could make a nice wall hanging. She spread it wide. "Gary, what do you think of this?"

His gaze darted between the scarf and her. "I think the greens look nice with your red hair."

"Autumn, do you..." Susan whipped her head around, checking in every direction. She couldn't see her daughter anywhere. Her heart pounded, and her breath stalled in her throat. Every bright red shirt she spotted belonged to somebody else. She dropped the scarf on the table.

Gary grabbed her hand. "She must have kept walking."

Surely, a kidnapping couldn't go unnoticed in this crowd. But she remembered times where a parent dragged a kid away from a park, and the kid screamed bloody murder. She wouldn't have known if it was a kidnapping. No! It wasn't happening.

"She's lost in the crowd." He darted around a dawdling couple, and she swerved to miss them. She imagined sirens and lights attached to the top of Gary's head like a police car so the crowd would move aside and let them pass. His panicked, "Excuse me," did the trick.

Susan's head swiveled from side to side, checking each seller's stall and trying to see behind every adult. No red t-shirt. Unless a kidnapper had pulled a different one on over it. She didn't need to think of that.

They were nearing the end of the vendors. Beyond, a wide field opened up. The crowd was more dispersed, but it was a bigger area to search.

Gary squeezed her hand. "I just got a glimpse of her. She's standing by the last canopy."

Susan couldn't see her daughter yet, but raised her voice. "Autumn!" The relief that washed over her left her feeling weak.

Gary frantically waved. "She saw me." He continued pushing through the crowd, dragging her behind, until they stopped in front of her daughter.

Susan hugged her tight, then pushed her back, hands on her shoulders. "You're supposed to stay with us."

Susan's fear of what could have happened overrode her ability to calm down.

The girl bit her lip. "Mom, I was, but you stopped and I didn't notice. Then people were all around me and I couldn't see which way to go."

"I was so worried." Susan hugged Autumn again, her heart finally slowing. "I'm sorry. I should have said I was stopping."

Gary's arms came around both of them. He'd been worried, too. She couldn't help but compare him to Brian, who would have let Susan look for Autumn alone. Gary's lips skimmed the side of her head.

She met his gaze. "Thank you." She should say more, but she couldn't. Instead, she tipped up her head and kissed him, hoping that conveyed what her words didn't.

She wrapped an arm around her daughter's shoulders. "Let's go see what fun things they have for kids."

They headed toward the squeal of children, all holding hands. She smiled at Gary over Autumn's head, feeling like the three of them made up a family.

~~~

They headed back to Gary's car, and he could finally relax his vigilance. He'd been stressed since they'd lost Autumn. He'd been on missing children calls. It had never been as intense and scary as this. Today was the first time he'd spent any amount of time with Autumn, but he'd developed an attachment to her over the time he and Susan talked about her.

At the car, he stopped Susan from getting in while Autumn buckled up. "Can you show me where Brian lived? Then we can go get dinner."

"Okay. Don't ask Autumn what she wants or we'll end up at a burger place. How about Zentaro's? She loves their pizza, but they've got a full menu."

"Sounds perfect."

They got in the car and she gave directions. He paused at a stop sign.

"I can't remember if we turned left here or at the next stop sign."

Gary took the turn. "Let's try here. You'll know soon enough if it's wrong."

They traveled three blocks, then Susan shook her head. "No. It's not right."

"Good enough." He turned around in a driveway and came back to where they'd turned, getting back on the other road. Two blocks up, he stopped at another stop sign. "Does this look right?"

"Yes. Left here."

After four blocks, he glanced at her, not expecting it to be this far.

She pointed. "There. It's the sign for the apartments."

A half block ahead, a long black sign with scrolled gold letters announced *Comstock Acres*. He turned into the driveway. There were eight buildings, four on each side of the parking lot. The exterior was well maintained. He couldn't understand why Jeffers wouldn't have invited Susan inside.

"What are we doing here?" Autumn asked.

Gary pulled into the nearest empty space. "We're just looking at something real quick, honey." He turned to Susan. "Do you remember which building?"

"That one." She pointed to the second in the back row, labeled building seven. "I didn't go in, so I don't know which unit."

"Okay. That's good enough. Thanks." He drove to the restaurant. He'd only eaten there once, on a date, and couldn't remember anything about it.

It was a nice way to finish their day.

~~~

Monday morning, Gary turned into the drive for Comstock Acres. The last time, he'd missed the small discreet sign giving the apartment manager's phone number and unit number. Being a weekday, more than half of the parking spaces were empty. He pulled into a spot in the center, parking nearest to building four, went inside, and easily found unit one. A label beside the door designated it belonged to the manager. He knocked.

The door opened, and a man with steel gray hair, and piercing blue eyes studied him. He wore jeans and a faded Metallica t-shirt. "You interested in an apartment?"

Gary showed his badge. "I'm interested in finding out what you know about a previous tenant. He would have left about three years ago."

"Not likely to remember that long ago." He indicated all the buildings. "We've got a lot of tenants."

"He used to live in building seven. Brian Jeffers."

The man's eyebrows rose. "The serial killer. I remember *him*. Lived with a woman."

Gary wasn't surprised the man would remember his infamous tenant.

"Did they seem like they were a couple or just roommates?"

The man folded his arms and leaned against the doorframe. "Neighbors complained they left their windows open when they went at each other. I had to tell them to close the windows. What do you think?"

Gary had to hide a smile. "At each other? You mean arguing or sex?"

"Yeah. The second. They were in your face about it. Walking out to the car, he'd have his hand under her shirt. Once saw him lean into the car and kiss her and stick his hand up her skirt. We have families living here. It's no place for that."

Normally, Gary would take notes, but he felt it would stop the flow of information if he started writing. This was more of a gossip kind of conversation. "What happened when he moved?"

"I thought they broke up. He helped her move to a smaller unit in building six. But he came back a couple times a week. During the day. The look on his face when he left, you could tell he got what he wanted."

He wondered if the woman knew Jeffers had started killing women.

Time for serious police work. "Does she still live here?"

"Yep."

"What's her name? Which unit?" Finally, he could talk to one of the women Jeffers had known.

"California Jackson. Six-twenty-one. That's the second floor."

It shouldn't have surprised him. Jeffers did talk to California at Bar to Nowhere. "Thank you. I'm going to talk to her. If she's not there, please don't tell her I'm looking for her."

"I'll keep quiet."

Gary strolled across the lot to building six, and took the stairs to the second floor. He knocked on the door and waited. Twice more he knocked with no response.

He'd have to come back. This was the only lead he had. Jeffers had moved in with Susan when they married, but all the while, Jeffers had kept this woman as his mistress. Susan deserved so much better than a man like that.

Chapter 9

Twice a week Susan went to lunch with coworkers. After the last message from her stalker, she wouldn't leave the building until the end of the day. Sack lunches were in her foreseeable future. Every day.

She dropped a contract into her briefcase and closed it.

She missed Gary. Which was crazy since she'd been with him all afternoon two days ago. Waving at him as she left her office and when she got home wouldn't be enough. She fished her cell phone from her purse and texted him. *Can you come in when you get to my house?*

It took only moments before a response came in. *Okay.*

She grinned, and collected her belongings, then headed for the door.

Wayne walked with her to her car. "Any news on this stalker?" he asked.

"No. But Gary's still following leads. What few there are. At least it's not like…" She didn't want to bring up Brian and how no leads in that case meant more women died.

Wayne rested his hand on her shoulder. "I'm sure he'll get it all figured out. In the meantime, you're being careful."

"As much as I can be. Thanks for walking me, Wayne." She opened her door, climbed in and locked it. He never walked away until the lock clicked.

He gave a thumbs up and turned back to the building.

She pulled onto the street and Gary fell in behind her.

When she'd texted him, she only half thought about what would happen. Who was she kidding? She totally wanted to kiss him until Autumn got home. Maybe she could invite him for dinner. And if he stayed long enough, after Autumn went to bed, they could find some alone time.

Susan pulled into the garage, unlocked the mudroom door and waited impatiently for Gary to park and join her.

She took his hand, dragged him inside and hit the security buttons. In the kitchen, she maneuvered them aside so that when the door opened, they'd be behind it. Gary tipped his head and lifted an eyebrow when she took his other hand. She'd wanted to attack him with kisses, and now she turned into a coward.

He slipped a hand from hers and skimmed it over the back of her neck. He touched his lips to hers and pulled back.

That gave her the encouragement she needed to follow through. She lifted to her toes and kissed him.

They were like teens in an empty classroom, knowing any moment the teacher or other students would walk in, and trying to go as far as they could. Autumn's voice in the garage penetrated her foggy brain, and she kissed Gary's cheek then stepped back. "Can you stay for dinner? I'm hoping we'll have some alone time after Autumn goes to bed at eight."

"I'd like that."

Then the door opened. It wasn't suspicious at all that they were right behind it. Autumn didn't notice anything strange, but Chris quirked a brow. And she didn't care. She deserved to enjoy time with a man. Especially this one.

Autumn dropped her backpack on the floor. "Gary. Are you eating with us?"

"I sure am, honey."

"Mom, can I sit beside Gary?"

It warmed her heart that Autumn and Gary truly liked each other. "Yes. Why don't you wash up and Gary can help you set the table?" Susan glanced at Gary and he grinned.

She turned to the bodyguard watching the scene. "Thanks, Chris. Following a kid around school must be a boring job for you."

"It's all right. And I end up with some funny stories for my kids about things that happen at school. Speaking of them, I better be on my way."

She smiled. "Have a good night. See you tomorrow."

She waited for Chris to leave then headed to the dining room to check on progress. They'd added a place setting beside Autumn's seat.

Autumn patted her chair. "And I want you to sit here, so you can sit beside Mom, too."

Her daughter was thoughtful to make sure she and Gary sat close. Maybe her nine-year-old daughter was matchmaking. It felt good that the man she was interested in was also liked by the rest of her family.

She continued into the kitchen and pulled dinner from the oven. Lasagna. She removed a towel that covered a basket of rolls and slid them into the oven and set the timer. A huge salad waited in the refrigerator.

Gary stepped behind her, gripped her upper arms and kissed the side of her neck. "It smells almost as delicious as you do. Is there anything else I can do to help?"

She melted a little. Anthony had been the only other man to give her this kind of simple affection. She hadn't realized how much she missed it. She scooted back, coming in contact with his chest. Even better.

"Where's Autumn?"

"She said something about if she finished her homework before dinner, you might let her swim after."

She chuckled. "That girl is a fish. Once she found out the junior high had a swim team, she's been swimming as much as possible. She's determined to make it on the team."

"Don't they take everybody?"

"Yes, but she thinks it's like the football team where they

have tryouts."

Susan stepped away from him just as Theo and Bradley walked through the kitchen door. She grabbed the salad and handed it to Gary. "Can you put this on the table? There's a salad set in the second drawer."

Bradley wiggled his eyebrows. "Dinner guest, huh?"

"Yes." She snapped a dishtowel at him. "Don't be like that."

Theo patted his brother's shoulder and yanked the dishtowel from her hands. "Yeah, just tell her to go for it."

If she still had the towel, she'd have snapped it at Theo, too. And he knew it.

He took her hand, his expression serious. "Dad would want you to be happy, and you haven't been for a long time." He nodded toward the dining room. "That guy in there, he puts a smile on your face—" He touched her temple. "—that reaches your eyes."

She turned and picked up the lasagna to give herself a chance to clear her misty eyes. She couldn't have asked for more caring stepsons.

Dinner was delicious, but with the loads of cheese Miriam used, it couldn't miss. It amazed Susan how easily Gary fit into the dinner conversation. First meal with all of them, and he carried it off as if he'd eaten with them dozens of times. Cleanup was accomplished quickly with everybody helping.

After Autumn stuck her plate in the dishwasher she gazed at Susan. "Mom, can I swim? My homework is all done." It was hard to resist the pleading in Autumn's eyes. She did swim two days before, but that was with Grace and they played around, not giving Autumn time for serious swimming.

Susan stared at Gary. She'd hoped to have a quiet evening before Autumn went to bed. Now, he might decide it would be best to leave. "Do you mind?"

"I'll come watch, if that's all right."

Theo grinned behind Gary. "There are clean swimsuits in

the changing room, if you want to join them.

Autumn jumped up and down. "Yes! Yes! Swim with us."

Gary smiled. "How can I refuse that?"

"I'll show you to the pool while the ladies change," Theo said.

Autumn scampered up the stairs and Susan followed.

Her daughter stopped in front of Susan's door. "Mom, I really like Gary. He's nicer than Brian. And when I was lost, and you two found me, he hugged us." She hugged Susan. Was she showing affection or demonstrating her enthusiasm for Gary?

Susan turned into her sitting room and headed straight to the bedroom, shutting the door. She was in a quandary over which swimsuit to wear. If she swam alone or with family, quite often, she wore a bikini. But if they had guests, she wore a one-piece. She did have that in between tankini.

Sometimes it didn't pay to have too many choices. She wavered for a minute more and finally snatched up the tankini then dropped it on her bed. As she tore off her clothes, the stampede of young feet passed her door. She drew on the swimsuit and wrapped a beach robe around her. At a more sedate pace, she headed to the pool.

Gary swam beside Autumn. He paused, somehow knowing Susan had arrived, turned, and his eyes widened when Susan took off her robe. She tingled in all the right places at his reaction.

He caught up with Autumn, and the two reached the end of the pool. Gary demonstrated an arm move and Autumn copied. It was nice that he helped improve her skills.

Susan dove in and sliced through the water until she reached them at the far side. "Mind if I race with you two?" Susan was more of a leisurely swimmer, which worked out well with Autumn. The winner tended to alternate, but Autumn was starting to edge ahead in the wins.

"Okay," Gary said. They all turned their backs to the wall.

"Call it, Autumn."

The girl yelled, "One, two, three, go!"

Water flew in all directions as they struck out for the other side. Gary was in the lead by a stroke, so he must have held back to swim beside Autumn. Whatever he'd shown her about her stroke, paid off. She was a body length ahead of Susan midway across the pool.

Susan glided in last, gasping. "That's enough racing for me."

"Gary, you were so fast! You should race Theo."

He chuckled. "I'm sure a man who has his own pool can swim faster than me."

Susan pushed away from the wall and swam on her back. "Why don't you two swim some more laps, and then we'll play."

They took off at a fast pace as Susan paddled around and relaxed.

After a few continuous laps, Gary and Autumn had a competition of who could create the biggest splash. After being drenched a couple of times, Susan kept her distance.

Theo strolled in. "Hey, shrimp. It's bedtime."

Susan swam to a ladder.

Theo waved her back. "No stay. I've got this."

Autumn pushed her bottom lip out. "Aw, Theo."

He grabbed a towel from a shelf. "Come on out. If you're fast getting ready, I'll read extra long to you."

Gary swam to Autumn. "Thanks for inviting me into the pool. I had a lot of fun. We'll have to do it again."

Autumn threw her arms around his neck. "Me, too. It was so fun." She scrambled from the pool.

Theo's hand was on Autumn's shoulder as they left.

Gary wrapped an arm around Susan's waist. "They're really close, aren't they?"

She nodded. "And Bradley, too. More so since Anthony died. They really stepped up to be father figures for her."

"It's nice she has them."

She wiggled free and stopped halfway up the ladder. "You want to go in the hot tub?"

He grinned. "I saw that in the corner. It sounds good."

Susan felt his gaze on her, and she tugged the bottom of her top into place as she strode to the hot tub. She hit the button on the wall to start the jets, then stepped into the warm, bubbly water and to the far side. She spun around and slowly lowered into the water and leaned back in the seat. The tub held ten people, but they hadn't had a pool party in over a year. Autumn wanted one for her birthday in a few months.

Gary paused on each step into the water, studying her face. Maybe he wondered how close he should sit. She lifted her arm out of the bubbles and patted the water beside her. One corner of his mouth kicked up, then he waded across and sat, touching shoulders. His hand rested on her thigh near her knee. Her heart beat faster with the hope he'd slide it higher, but she knew he wouldn't. Yet.

Gary sighed as he slid lower into the water. "Last time I got to do this I was on vacation."

"You don't belong to a gym with a pool?" He was in good shape with nice muscles, all the better to see in a swimsuit.

"I used to have a gym membership, but I bought a home gym. It saves time, and if I can't sleep in the middle of the night, I don't have to forgo exercise because the gym is closed. But I do miss swimming. The gym had a sauna but not a hot tub."

Susan pointed to a frosted glass door next to the changing room. "We have a sauna, too. It has to be turned on before your swim so it's hot enough when you're ready."

Gary lifted his arm and dropped it around her shoulder. "Thanks for inviting me in. I've had a nice evening. With those brothers who would do anything for her, Autumn could be spoiled, but she's a great kid."

Susan leaned her head into him. "She is, isn't she? She lost her father when she was five, but she sometimes talks about things they did together. A year or so ago, she did some internet searches on him, and found interviews and pictures. She saved them on her computer."

"At eight?"

She laughed. "Yeah. In one of Autumn's classes, the teacher showed them how to search some topic they were studying, and of course, she took it one step further."

"That's nice she has some way to keep him alive."

She shook her head. "I don't know why I'm telling you this."

He kissed the top of her head, and her heart squeezed. "You're proud of her. And maybe you want to remind me what a great guy your husband was."

She leaned back and stared up at him. "You think so?"

He shrugged. "I don't know, but I'm happy you had a loving relationship."

"Thank you." She sighed. "I expected to have a similar relationship with Brian."

"No two relationships are alike. Even if he'd been … normal, it would have been very different."

"He was loving at first. I didn't associate it at the time, but he changed when he found out I didn't inherit Anthony's money."

"How so?"

Susan liked how he showed just the right amount of curiosity. The interest of a friend, but not morbid curiosity. "I guess he didn't have to pretend to love me anymore. I didn't notice right away, but stopped kissing me hello and goodbye. I still did that. And, um, sex wasn't as satisfying or as often."

She started to pull away, but Gary hugged her tighter.

"He got what he wanted, but he didn't care about you?"

"Yes." She shivered. "And I hate thinking about how he had sex with me after raping those women."

"Shh. Don't think about that. It really had nothing to do

with you. It was insane rationalization in his own head."

She wrapped an arm around his waist. "I'd gotten good at forgetting about him, but he's the reason this crazy person wants me dead, so I can't keep him out of my head."

"Hey, does this place have a sound system?"

She jerked. "What?" That was quite the subject change, but maybe they needed it.

"I was just thinking about how we danced the other night, and I'd love to do it again, especially in our swimsuits."

That sounded amazing to her. "Yes, but not easily. We play music for parties, but it has to be set up."

"Mmm. So maybe a kiss instead." He shifted so he was on his knees in front of her. She parted her legs to let him get closer. He planted his hands on either side of her shoulders and leaned in. His lips touched the corner of her mouth, and she turned for a fuller kiss, but he kissed the other corner. "You're impatient."

In such a short time, she'd grown addicted to his kisses. She closed her eyes and rested her head against the wall of the hot tub. His lips trailed across her jaw to her neck, and she shivered. The good kind of shiver. The kind that made her want to wrap her body around his.

His lips came back to hers, and she ran her hands up his chest, along his neck and into his hair. His tongue twined with hers, and she wished their bodies were touching. He trailed kisses down her neck, sending sensual messages to southern parts of her body, making her want to strip off her swimsuit. And his.

The jets turned off and Gary pulled back, his breathing heavy. The water was clear now, revealing his body's desire for her.

He blew out a long breath. "Maybe we should jump back into the pool to cool off."

Susan didn't want to stop kissing, but was she really ready for the next step?

Gary spun and climbed out of the water. She couldn't take her eyes off him as he strode across the floor and executed a shallow dive into the pool. It probably had a better effect than a cold shower.

She climbed out and across the floor, then plunged feet first into the pool. The water instantly cooled her skin. As she floated slowly to the surface, the heat seeped out of her body. Her head bobbed up and she sucked in a huge breath.

Gary's arms came around her and he maneuvered them to the nearest wall. He grabbed the wall with one hand and kissed her. She wrapped her arms around his neck, trusting him to keep their heads above water. Apparently, the cold shower effect hadn't worked.

He snuggled his head next to hers. "I think I should leave before I do something I shouldn't. Why don't we get dressed?"

She was of two minds about ending their evening, but he was right. She didn't want to regret anything with Gary. "Okay. My clothes are in my room."

"I don't want to wander alone through your house, so why don't you come back here after you change?"

"All right." She grabbed a couple towels from a shelf near the changing room and handed him one. She couldn't resist kissing him once more, before drying and slipping on her robe. She glanced up and found him watching her.

"I wish I'd done that."

She frowned. "Done what?"

"Run the towel all over your body."

"Oh." If she wasn't cold from the plunge in the pool, she would have blushed. "See you in ten minutes." She fled to her bedroom. It was all too easy to imagine Gary drying her, then removing her swimsuit to dry under it, too.

In her bathroom, she removed her suit and rinsed it in the sink, then hung it over the shower door. She stepped into the shower and let the warm water wash away the salt then dried again, combed out her hair, and contemplated what she should wear. She couldn't very well put on pajamas, like she normally did after a late swim. Maybe jeans, but she wanted to be more comfortable. Leggings and a t-shirt would do. Too bad she'd have to wear a bra.

Susan went back to the pool and found Gary on a lounger, studying his phone.

"Hi."

He stood. "I had a good evening."

She took his hand. "Me, too."

He pulled her closer, but not close enough that their bodies touched, and kissed her forehead.

He stared into her eyes, so close she saw a small speck of brown in one blue iris. "It's getting late. But how about going out to dinner on Thursday?"

She smiled. "I'd like that."

"Okay. I'll follow you home like last time, and we'll leave from here. How about Jackie Rae's?"

"Sounds good. I can run in and change."

He took her hand, and they left the pool area. "You'll have to lead the way. I'd be guessing."

"I didn't keep you away from anything tonight, did I?"

He released her hand and wrapped his arm around her back. "Only a phone call from you, and this was better."

"You didn't mind spending time with Autumn?"

"She's a great kid. You could tell I was having fun, right?"

She laughed. "Yes. It's just that some people pretend with kids."

They'd reached the front door, and he turned her into his arms, and waited until she stared into his eyes to speak. "I was being genuine. Autumn's special, and I'm not saying that because I have any ulterior motives. I enjoy being with both of you."

After the fair on Saturday, she'd thought he liked kids, but that was different than becoming a parent to one who wasn't your own. Her heart opened wider. "I'm looking forward to dinner on Thursday."

She wrapped her arms around the back of his neck and touched her lips to his. Gary's kisses made her forget everything except wanting to explore more of him.

He pulled back. "I really have to go."

"Okay."

He gave her a last slow kiss, as if he couldn't leave without touching her once more, then he slipped out the door. She blew out a long breath. It would be hard to wait for Thursday, but at least they'd talk before then.

Chapter 10

Gary left the station early, went home, and changed into jeans before driving to Susan's work. He was looking forward to dinner. They'd talked on the phone Wednesday evening, but it wasn't the same as being with her——watching the expressions that crossed her face and touching her beautiful body.

He turned into the parking lot and drove his normal circuit, checking for anything suspicious. He paused behind Susan's car and inched forward. Two flat tires on the side she wouldn't see. Definitely vandalized. He swore and pulled in beside her car. He got out and examined them more closely. Both had been punctured, likely with a knife.

The security guard would have dropped Susan at her car and left after she was safely locked inside. She wouldn't have discovered until she tried to drive away that the tires were flat. The stalker might have attacked or taken her when she stepped out to investigate. The last stalker message had said "Times up." This might have been a perfect setup.

Susan came around the building with Wayne, a frown on her face. They reached her car. "What's wrong?"

"You have two flat tires." He glanced at the other man. "Thanks for bringing her out, Wayne. I've got it from here."

"You're sure?"

"Yes, but can you review the security video for today?"

Wayne nodded. "Sure thing. As soon as I get inside." He returned to the building.

He opened his car door and nudged her into the protective space between the door and the car. "Why don't you call Mike? And maybe see if Theo or Bradley can meet Autumn and Chris at home."

She bit her lip, the skin tight around her eyes. She pulled her cell phone from her purse. Her voice rose in pitch speaking to Mike, asking him to pick up her car. Her defeated expression and the slump of her shoulders broke Gary's heart. Next, she called Theo and explained what happened and asked him to be home for Autumn. Then she asked if he minded if she still spent the evening with Gary. She tucked her phone away.

He hadn't expected she would still want to have their night together, but was glad she did.

"Let's get you in the car." He took her to the other side and closed the door after she was seated. He snapped a couple pictures of her car and the flat tires, and joined her. "I need to check what Wayne found."

He drove to the building and parked beside the office door then they went inside. Nobody manned the desk, but Wayne peeked out the security door. Gary held Susan's trembling hand and led her to the small room. "Find anything, Wayne?"

Wayne pointed at the screen. "Just like last time. No face showed. Here, I stopped the action as the guy entered the screen." He backed away, giving Gary space to take a seat.

Gary sat and Susan stood behind his shoulder. He hit play and watched the perp advance on Susan's car, one hand in a black hoodie pocket, head covered and bowed. Once reaching the car, a knife was taken from the pocket and the blade opened. The slashed tires were on the opposite side of the car from the camera, so the stalker ducked out of sight. Then the figure walked to the rear of the car and leaned down. The stalker sprinted for the back of the parking lot.

The video was little help. They never got a look at the face. The perp's build was slim like last time and could be a woman. The bulky hoodie made it hard to tell for sure.

Gary stood. "Wayne, can you send this?" Hopefully, Dave could see more than Gary.

"I'll get that to you ASAP."

"Thanks, Wayne."

Gary touched Susan's back. "Let's go. How about if we pick up some food and go back to my place to eat?" It might be too intimate for her, but he didn't think it was a good idea to be at a public restaurant right after the flat tire scare.

"Okay."

"I need to stop at the station to file a report first." He drove to the police station, and Susan sat in a chair beside his desk. First he went online and ordered food for pickup. Then he logged in the information regarding the damage to Susan's car, including the pictures he'd taken. He shut down his computer and stood.

"All set. Let's go."

After he picked up the food, they arrived at Gary's house. He was relieved he'd cleaned the place on the remote possibility that Susan would come home with him after they had dinner. They kicked off their shoes, and he seated her at the kitchen table. He set the bags in front of her then lit a candle in a jar, and dimmed the lights, hoping for a romantic and relaxing dinner.

He set the table and pulled a bottle of wine from the refrigerator that he'd purchased specifically for this evening. He opened the containers and stuck serving spoons in them.

Susan wrapped a hand around his upper arm and kissed his cheek. "Thank you for doing this. I feel safe here with you."

Gary hated that she'd felt unsafe, but was glad he could offer her safety. He sat diagonally from her and scooped up some potatoes. "Even after your car is fixed, I think your stepsons should drop you off at work, and I'll take you home. There's no sense risking that stalker getting close to you."

"You're right. I just wish this was over."

He squeezed her hand. "I'm still following one lead. Brian

used to be with California Jackson. I've stopped several times to see her, but she hasn't been home."

"Do you think she's the one doing this?"

He shrugged. "Maybe. He was with her before he married you." And during, but he wouldn't mention that. "If she still loves him, she might think he'd still be alive if he hadn't married you."

Her eyes widened. "That might be true. Not that I had anything to do with what he did."

Susan didn't die, but she was one of Jeffers' victims, too.

They talked of other things through the rest of the meal, then put away leftovers.

Gary held out his hand. "Come sit with me in the living room." Her warm hand fit into his, and he led her to the stereo and pushed the button. Soft music played, the first of the many songs he'd cued up earlier. He sat on the middle cushion of the couch, bought for comfort and not looks, and drew her into his side. She laid her head on his shoulder. He wouldn't mind doing this every night after dinner.

He lifted her hand and kissed the back of it. "This is so much better than talking on the phone."

"Is this where you sit when we talk?"

He nodded toward his recliner. "Usually there, but I didn't think you'd want to sit on my lap." He grinned at her blush and kissed her temple. "Sometimes, I'm in bed."

"Me, too." Her voice was a whispered breath against his skin in the open collar of his shirt.

That was something he could imagine the next time they talked on the phone. Though, he might have trouble getting through the call.

He tipped her chin up and kissed her as he dragged her legs across his lap so she wouldn't have to twist her neck. Her hand slipped up his chest to his shoulder and onto the side of his neck. He leaned back and gazed at her for a few seconds, giving her a chance to make the decision. She pulled his head back down and kissed him.

Gary had been attracted to her from the first moment he saw her. The more time he spent with her, the greater his appreciation of her ability to deal with what life threw her way. And the more he discovered her soft side.

Susan shifted her legs to the floor and stood. He rubbed a hand down his face. It *was* getting late. Then she straddled his lap, wrapped her arms around his neck and kissed him. He was all for it. He slouched in the seat, all the better to have full torso contact. Her heat enveloped him and he moaned.

He slid one hand into her hair and the other pulled her lower back tighter against him. He wished she'd worn a skirt, hiked up high on her legs, but the thin fabric of her dress pants wouldn't shield her from his obvious reaction to her kisses.

He twisted and tipped to the side, dropping flat on his back, taking her with him, then swung his legs up onto the couch. Susan squeaked, but resumed kissing him. Her hand slipped between them and rubbed over his nipple. He moaned and ground into her.

She set off all kinds of wants and longing inside him, not just for her body. Any time spent with her was time well spent. Watching her animated face when she talked about something she loved—especially Autumn, holding her hand while they walked, kissing her goodnight, or doing this. All were special because of her.

He showered her cheek, jaw and neck with kisses then dropped his head. He slid his hands to the middle of her back. Her fast paced breathing matched his. He struggled with himself not to go further tonight. He didn't want their first time to be sullied by the stalker.

She gave him a quick kiss and grinned. "I liked that. I'm not sure why you stopped."

He rubbed the back of her neck. "You've had a rough evening. Next time, I might not be able stop. Why don't I take you home now?"

She stared at him. "Okay. I enjoyed this evening. All of it." Her eyes sparkled.

He helped her up and kissed her. "You make it hard to be a gentleman."

She hugged him. "Maybe I don't want a gentleman."

"I'll remember that for next time."

~~~

Gary had stopped by California's apartment at different times of the day without luck. This time, he arrived at six-thirty in the morning. Likely, she was still in bed, but at least, she'd be there. He hoped.

He gave her door some quick raps and waited. No sound inside. He knocked harder. If she was still sleeping, it might take more to rouse her. A third time, he knocked and the door behind him opened. He spun around.

A bleary-eyed man ran a hand through his hair. "You know what time it is?"

"Sorry." Gary flipped his badge open. "I've tried all times of the day to talk to Miss Jackson, but she hasn't been home."

The man rubbed his jaw. "I hadn't seen her for a few days, so I think she was away. We don't talk, so I don't know for sure. Last night, I saw her come in when I was taking trash out to the dumpster."

Gary pointed a thumb over his shoulder. "So, she's in now?"

The guy shrugged. "Likely. She doesn't seem to be a morning person."

"Thanks. Sorry I woke you, but I'm going to keep trying."

Gary turned back to the door, and the one behind him closed. He wondered where California had been and if it was important. He knocked harder and longer than the last time. "Miss Jackson, I need to talk to you."

Something inside scraped, maybe a chair on the floor. She

was still home.

The door opened just wide enough to see a blonde woman with blue streaks in her hair glare at him. One hand wrapped around the door at head height and the other was planted on her hip. "What do you want at the crack of dawn?"

He showed his badge. "I need to ask some questions about Brian Jeffers. May I come in?"

She shook her head, and her chin quivered. "He's dead."

"Did you date him?"

"Why should I tell you?"

Gary shrugged one shoulder. "I don't see why you wouldn't."

"Yeah, so what?"

"Maybe you blame someone for his death."

Her eyes narrowed. "He committed suicide."

Gary couldn't get a read on her. She didn't want to talk to him, but he got that a lot when he questioned people. "Do you think someone pushed him into doing it?"

"You mean like, told him he should kill himself?" Her breathing was slow and even, maybe too controlled. "No." Her knuckles on the door had turned white.

Gary studied her. "More like made him see he was going to prison, and he couldn't take it."

She shrugged.

His next question could have a myriad of responses. "Did you know Brian was killing women?" California hadn't been present when Shannon had been rescued, so likely she hadn't been present when the others were killed.

She pursed her lips. "I don't think he did it." Her response wasn't as strong as saying, 'He didn't do it,' but her expression and words shouted that she wanted to believe he hadn't.

"He was caught as he was about to rape the last victim. She was tied to a bed at the lake house his family owned and there was an X-Acto blade on the table beside him. Tell me how anyone else could have been responsible."

Her eyes sparkled with unshed tears. She stepped back, and slammed the door then locked it.

He'd pushed too hard, and didn't know if he'd accomplished anything. Maybe instead of forcing her to realize Jeffers was a serial killer, he should have asked her if she knew he had wanted to kill Susan for her money. If she'd known, that would make her an accomplice, but she wouldn't have been likely to admit it.

He rubbed a hand over his face and trudged back to his car, still in a quandary over where California fit into this. Was she responsible for stalking Susan? Was Jeffers' sister? Did California know Callista?

~~~

That night, Susan checked to make sure Autumn was asleep before retiring to her room. She changed and climbed under her bed covers. A couple of times, she'd talked to Gary while sitting, fully clothed on her bed. This was the first time she'd done anything like this, and it made her feel sensuous. He didn't have to know where she was or how she was dressed.

She propped up a pillow and leaned back then called his number.

"Hey, beautiful."

"Hi, Gary." It was sort of embarrassing the way he made her believe she was beautiful when he said it. She drew her knees up to her chest.

It had been nice being picked up by him after work. They'd talked, and she'd given him a goodbye kiss before going inside. It was too short and sweet. She wanted more.

"How's Autumn?"

"Good. She's enjoying having her own bodyguard, but I hope we can get back to normal soon."

"I finally talked to California Jackson today. I didn't get very far."

"How come?" She'd pinned her hopes on California.

"She doesn't believe Brian killed those women."

"Seriously? He was caught red-handed."

"I told her how he was caught. She got teary and slammed the door in my face."

Susan felt a bit sorry for the woman. She'd started to become disillusioned by her husband by the time he died, but California probably loved him to the end. "Will you go back and talk to her?"

"I might. I still want to ask her if she knows Brian's sister."

"What was her name?"

"Callista."

She sat up straighter. "You know, that's kind of strange."

"What is?"

"Both names would have a nickname of Callie. And both last names start with a J."

Gary whistled. "I didn't make the connection. California's ID at *Bar to Nowhere* had the wrong number, and could have been an error, but was likely fake."

"But why would she try to pass as his girlfriend rather than his sister? She wasn't in trouble with the law, was she?"

"She doesn't have a record. She seemed to have disappeared. This would explain it."

She leaned against the headboard. "So why the lie?"

"Freedom to have sex without offending their neighbors? The landlord said that sometimes they had sex with the windows open."

"Ew. His sister?" She'd been married to a man who had sex with his sister. Of course, that wasn't worse than him being a rapist-killer.

"Technically, half-sister, but same thing."

"Do you think she's the same person? I would have leaned toward that, but not after hearing about them having sex." She shivered. "Were they...together after I married Brian?"

Silence. She waited a few more seconds. "Okay. That answers my question."

"I'm sorry, Susan. The landlord said he still visited her after he moved out."

"Can we talk about something else, so I don't have that on my mind when I go to sleep?"

"Of course. How about setting up another date?"

"Do you want to go to the lake on Saturday? Theo and Bradley moved the boat a couple days ago and unpacked the dishes. There's no furniture yet, but a picnic table and grill are being delivered tomorrow."

"That sounds fun. Thank you."

"Autumn has invited a couple friends, so it might get a bit noisy."

"That's fine. The guys going to be there, too?"

"Theo is. I'm not sure about Bradley. Do you want to meet us there?"

"All right. What's the address?"

"Detective Wassman doesn't know already?" She laughed.

"I could find out, but it would be easier if you told me."

She gave him the address. "Bring your swim trunks. The lake's not warm enough to stay in long yet, but we'll probably get in. And there are the kayaks, too."

"Sounds fun. I'll see you tomorrow."

"Goodnight, Gary."

"Goodnight, beautiful."

Susan set the phone on the nightstand. Talking with him before going to sleep was nice, but being in his arms like the night before while they talked was better. The way Gary cared for her safety, the long talks on the phone, and everything she found out about him she liked. The way he interacted with Autumn. The way he kissed her like he really meant it. After her wonderful first marriage, and the fiasco of a second, she didn't think she'd ever have the chance of finding love again. But she recognized her feelings for Gary were growing into love, and it shocked her that he'd snuck into her heart.

Chapter 11

Susan beached her kayak beside Gary's double. Fun and sun at the lake house had been a much appreciated respite.

Autumn had already jumped out and twirled around. "That was so much fun. And we beat you, Mom."

"It doesn't count when it's two against one." Of course, one-on-one with Gary, she still would have lost. His powerful arms wielding a paddle could propel him through the water faster than her arms could.

Gary stepped out of his kayak, and Autumn gave him a quick hug before running off. Autumn's friends had made the day exciting. The girls splashed in the water and encouraged everybody to play volleyball. They'd eaten an early dinner—hamburgers, corn on the cob, and potato salad—before the girls' parents picked them up. That's when Gary suggested kayaking to occupy Autumn.

Susan ran a hand down Gary's back. "One reason why I lost—"

"You mean, besides two-to-one?"

"Yeah." She kissed his cheek and whispered in his ear. "Because it was so sexy watching your back muscles flex while you paddled so hard."

He blushed and gave her a quick peck on the lips. They pulled their kayaks to the side of a small shed and flipped them over. At the other house, they had a rack to hold six kayaks. The family could afford to buy a new one. It was her fault there were so many expenses with selling and buying houses because she married the wrong man.

Gary wrapped his arms around her. "I don't like the look on your face. Whatever you're thinking about, stop."

She leaned her head on his chest. "Easier said than done. We wouldn't have had to buy another lake house if I hadn't married Brian."

"And if you could have had premonitions, you wouldn't have married him." He lifted her chin. "Honey, by word and deed he told you he loved you. This isn't your fault."

"I don't know why you're so understanding." She loved the skin-to-skin contact in their swimsuits, warmed by the sun and slick from exertion.

He kissed her cheek. "Because I've gotten to know you, and I love you."

Her eyes widened, and she held him tighter. This. There wasn't any part of her that doubted he meant it. "I love you, too." Her toes sunk into the sand as she pushed up to kiss him. Declaring their love should be a momentous occasion, but it flowed smoothly along with their growing relationship. She whispered in his ear. "I want to go home with you."

He pulled her closer, showing her he knew what she was asking for. His warm hand dove through her hair. "I want that, too." He kissed her hard and long. It would be torture waiting until they got to his place. "Do you need to take Autumn home?"

"No. Theo and Bradley can take her."

By the time they made it to the house, everything had been packed up, and her family was gone. She propped her fists on her hips. "I don't think I like that Theo and Bradley can read my mind. But let me call Theo to make sure they have her." She pulled her phone from her beach bag.

A message from Theo waited. *Autumn is with us. See you tomorrow.*

"Oh, my God." She showed the screen to Gary.

He chuckled. "I think they saw us kissing and decided to give us some space."

She grinned. "Your place?" She waved her hand behind her. "We could use my room here, but there's no bed or food and we'd have to make the long drive after." And she wanted their first time in his bed.

"We can go to my place."

She threw on a beach cover-up—no sense dressing when it would all come off once they got to his house.

Gary pulled on a t-shirt, grabbed their bags, and took her hand.

On the drive back, Gary kept his hand on Susan's bare leg, and hers was on his thigh. She scooted her hand higher, but he grabbed it and placed it near his knee. She understood. He was a cop and wouldn't allow himself to drive while distracted. She slid her hand to the inside of his thigh and barely touched his skin as she skimmed it higher. She reached his danger zone, and rubbed back down to his knee. Then repeated.

If she thought she could get away with it, she'd reach between the edges of his unbuttoned shirt and run her hand over his chest which was heaving as if he were running. His hand squeezed her thigh. She dropped her gaze to his shorts— definitely having an effect. Once they got to his place, there would be no stops on the way to the bedroom.

He turned into his driveway. "It felt like it took forever to get here." They got out of the car, and he grabbed their bags. He unlocked the door, and dropped the bags as soon as they stepped inside.

Gary closed the door and pushed her up against it, then his lips came down on hers. She'd thought their kisses were hot before, but this one was nearly out of control. He wouldn't be backing off this time. And she was oh, so ready.

His fingers flew over the three buttons of her cover-up then pushed it off her shoulders. There was a tug on the strings on her top before it dropped to the floor. He cupped her breasts and kissed each one. "Beautiful."

Susan found the tie inside Gary's swimsuit and yanked it loose. Then she hooked her fingers at his hips and pushed the suit down. It got hung up in front, and she slid a hand over him and worked the trunks loose.

He sucked in a breath and grabbed her hand, kissing it. No erogenous zones there, but it sent an arrow to her heart. She wiggled out of the bottom of her swimsuit, and it joined the heap on the floor. They were both naked. It was a new experience to be so caught up in touching each other's bodies that they had to strip just inside the door.

He picked her up. With one arm slung around his shoulders, Susan ran her other hand over his muscled chest and abs. She'd wanted to do it all day, but couldn't with everyone else around. She rubbed her thumb back-and-forth over his nipple.

Gary inhaled sharply and kissed her. He walked through the living room and down a hall. At his bed, Susan pulled back the covers and leaned back on the mattress.

Gary lowered himself on top of her, resting most of his weight on his forearms as he kissed her. "I've been dreaming about this."

She ran her hands up and down his back. The muscles flexed as he moved to her neck, then down to her nipple and drew it into his mouth. She gasped and slid one hand into his hair. A burst of hunger shot to her sex and she tipped her pelvis up into him. She thought he'd rush once they hit the bed, but he slowed down, as if needing to memorize every place he touched.

His hand slipped between them and he caressed her, sending a throbbing signal to her brain to shut down any thought except the pleasure he was imparting. His lips returned to hers as his fingers worked their magic. It had been too many years since she'd felt this much passion. Her body was overwhelmed with sensations. She kissed him harder, deeper, and her love for him overflowed her heart and filled her.

Tingles started slow, but built rapidly. She tensed as he discovered a most receptive spot. She screamed as she flew apart. Their heavy breathing filled the room. She hadn't noticed it before now.

He ripped open a condom, rolled it on then entered her. They moaned in unison. He started a slow rhythm, his breath fanning her ear. He kept most of his weight off her, but each move brushed his body against her. After a few strokes, the intensity returned, and she met his every thrust. Her lips brushed his neck, and she tasted pure Gary. As the pleasure mounted, she pushed her mouth against his neck to hold in a scream. Together they reached their peak, and he collapsed onto her for a moment before flipping them to their sides.

Gary peppered kisses over Susan's face. "That was…incredible."

She snuggled closer to the man she loved, every muscle relaxed. "I thought so, too."

Chapter 12

Susan sat in her office, a case book open beside her. She took notes on precedence for a disputed property. Her phone chimed with a text message. She finished the note and opened the messages. Autumn. Sometimes on her way to the after-school program, she'd send a message.

She clicked on Autumn's name and gasped, her heart flipped and picked up with an erratic beat. The text was a picture of Autumn tied to a chair with tape covering her mouth. The fear and tears in her daughter's eyes brought tears to her own. Dread twisted her insides so tight she could hardly breathe.

She closed her eyes and clutched her chest. If Autumn was going to survive this, Susan had to be strong. She drew in a long breath and stared at the screen.

If you want her set free, come to this address. Alone or she dies.

Her fingers trembled typing the message. *Don't hurt her.* This was all Susan's fault. She'd brought this danger to Autumn. If Susan didn't reach her soon enough, her daughter would pay the price.

The street name popped up. *Follow the rules.*

She'd had a house closing on that street, but she didn't know where it was. She texted back. *I don't have my car.* She should have insisted that she drive herself, but instead, she'd thought of her own safety. Now Autumn was in trouble.

Rich princess never taken a bus?

Susan had grown up taking buses. *Where?*

Get on the bus that stops at your building. Off on Washington. Go right and walk two blocks. Left and walk to address. No cops or she dies.

Susan typed, *OK*

Her association with Brian had caused Autumn to face something no little girl should have to. Susan would do anything to protect her daughter, even give up her own life.

She wished she could call Gary, but she couldn't risk Autumn's life.

Susan dropped her phone into her purse and rushed out the door. She didn't want to wait for the elevator and flew down the three flights of stairs, then out the exterior doors. She scanned the street until she found the bus stop sign. Two women stood beside it.

The bus hadn't come yet. Soon, she'd be there to protect Autumn. She might not survive this confrontation, but she'd make sure her daughter did.

~~~

Gary's cell phone rang. Chris Billings. His skin prickled and his shoulders tensed. Only bad news would force his call. "What's happening with Autumn, Chris?"

"Some woman took her. I'm sorry. She came out of the school behind us. She said Autumn had left something behind. We stopped and she tased me. Took my car keys and Autumn."

Gary grunted and slumped. He couldn't let Susan's daughter die. Neither of them deserved that. "Do you have a tracker on your car?"

"Yes. I'm calling it in as soon as we're done."

"Keep me informed."

"I will. I'm sorry."

"No need to be." He disconnected and tried Susan's number. After a few rings, it went to voicemail, and he asked her to call him. His roiling stomach told him she wouldn't be returning his call. This kidnapper knew that the way to get to Susan was through her daughter. He might lose both of them.

He hurried to Luke's office. "Hey, boss. Autumn Argyle's been kidnapped." Saying it out loud made it more real. He couldn't imagine how this would affect her.

Luke sucked in a breath and straightened his shoulders. The man had a daughter and a baby on the way. He'd know exactly how it felt for a child to go missing. "Send me her picture and I'll get an Amber Alert out."

Gary lifted his phone and sorted through some photos he'd taken at the beach and sent one to Luke. "I'm so frazzled, I didn't even think of that. Thanks. Her bodyguard is tracking his car, which the kidnapper used to get away. I'll keep you updated."

His office phone rang. "Hold on." He rushed to pick it up. "Detective Wassman."

"Detective, this is Wayne from Susan Argyle's building. She just ran out of here without looking at me. She was crying. She went to the bus stop and got on a minute ago."

"Which way did it go?"

"West."

"Thanks for calling, Wayne. That's a big help." The kidnapper had taken Autumn to draw Susan out. It gave a direction to start in, and by the time Chris had a location, Gary would be that much closer.

He hung up and returned to Luke's office. "That was security at Susan's office. He saw her leave by bus. I'm headed out now. Can you back me up?" Maybe Luke could go the lone hero route in rescuing Shannon, but Gary wanted every advantage to get Susan and Autumn back alive.

~~~

Only determination to rescue her daughter gave Susan the strength to put one foot in front of the other. A "For Sale" sign was stuck in the overgrown front lawn of the address she was given. She climbed the stairs and peeked in the living room window—no furniture. Her hand trembled as she raised it and knocked on the door.

A woman with obviously bleached blonde hair, the roots dark and unkempt, opened the door and stood back. Her eyes were shaped like Brian's, but maybe a bit darker. She had to be his sister.

"Where's Autumn?"

"Come on in. I've been looking forward to meeting you face-to-face."

Not a meeting Susan ever expected to have. "Are you Callista?" Maybe Susan knowing her name would throw the woman off balance. Or maybe it wasn't a good idea to stir up an unbalanced woman.

"Yes."

For all Susan knew, the woman had killed her daughter after taking the picture. Her stomach clenched so tight she thought she might throw up. For Autumn, she had to hold it together. "I want you to release Autumn now."

The woman grinned. "Of course, you do. But not yet."

"I need to see her."

Callista pointed with a knife similar to the one stabbed into the rabbit. "Through there."

Susan was fearful the crazy woman would plunge the knife into her back when she preceded Callista into the other room, but she'd have to risk it if she wanted to free Autumn.

Autumn sat in a chair in the center of the kitchen. Her eyes widened as Susan hurried toward her and squatted. She carefully peeled the tape off her mouth. Her daughter appeared to be unharmed. Her heart eased a bit, but Autumn was still in danger. The insane woman could go ballistic any moment.

"Mom, she hurt Chris." Her wonderful daughter, so often thinking of others before herself.

"I'm sure he's okay." She stood, kissed her daughter's

forehead, and faced the kidnapper. "You've got me now. Please, let her go."

The woman held a rope in her other hand. "Not yet. First we tie you up so you can't escape with her."

Susan instantly held her hands out. If she got the chance, she could head butt the woman.

"Turn around."

She complied. It would be harder to help Autumn with her hands behind her back, but she'd do what she could.

The knife clattered onto the counter. Now would be the time to take action, but Susan was too afraid that if she didn't succeed in taking down Callista, Autumn would pay the price. She had to take the chance the woman was telling the truth.

After her wrists were bound, Callista pointed to a chair six feet from Autumn. "Sit there."

Susan sat, her hands preventing her from leaning into the back.

The woman climbed onto the island and threaded a looped rope—a noose—through a large eye on the ceiling. She really did intend for Susan to die by the same method Brian had. She jumped to the floor and put the noose over Autumn's head.

Susan's heart pounded and she sprang to her feet. Her daughter needed to live. "No! You said you'd let her go if I came."

The woman chuckled. "That, I did." She narrowed her eyes and pointed at Susan. "Sit!" She removed the noose and looped it over Susan's head. She picked up the other end and tied it around the door lever handle. "There we go. You can't do anything without strangling yourself."

Callista untied the rope holding Autumn to the chair.

Susan hoped that meant her daughter would go free. She wouldn't believe it until Autumn was out the door. All her fear now was for her daughter. She'd accepted her own life as forfeited.

"Stand."

Autumn stood on trembling legs.

The woman freed Autumn's hands. "Say goodbye to your mother."

Autumn flung herself at Susan, nearly unseating her, and clung. "Mom, I'm afraid. I don't want to leave you."

Susan wanted to be strong, but couldn't stop the tears. Autumn would have nightmares for years, having to walk away from her mother, knowing she would die.

"You have to, honey. Go outside. Turn right and make another right at the corner. Go to the busy street and turn left. Then walk a long way until you get to my office. Right and right then left. I love you."

"Mom!"

"Do it!" Susan didn't want her last words to Autumn to be harsh, but her daughter's life was more important than Autumn's last memories of her.

Callista yanked Autumn's arm. "Time to go, little girl." She dragged her to the front door. Had she positioned the chair so Susan could see all the way there? She pulled the door open and shoved the girl out, then slammed and locked it.

The woman returned to the kitchen. "If she's still there when I'm done with you, it'll be her turn."

Susan wished she could see through the door to know that Autumn had left. She stared up at the woman. There must have been a small amount of compassion in her to have released Autumn. "Thank you for letting her go."

She shrugged. "I did it for Brian. I wanted him to kill her so you'd inherit her money, but he wouldn't do it. He said people shouldn't kill kids." She widened her stance and crossed her arms. "Our dad killed our older brother, when he was nine, in front of Brian."

"How old was Brian?" That must have been traumatic. He'd never mentioned a brother dying. Maybe that was the beginning of his mental problems.

"He was seven."

"Why wasn't your father arrested for murder?"

"He hid the body so well that nobody found it. Then he reported Tommy missing."

Susan didn't see her parents much, but they loved her and she couldn't imagine growing up with anything less. That twisted man had made his children as sick as him.

Callista jabbed a finger at Susan. "You were supposed to have money so he could take care of me like he wanted."

"Then he should have gone to school instead of trying to take a shortcut."

"Yeah, says the rich girl."

"I wasn't rich. I got school loans. Even if I hadn't married a rich man, I still would have made it through school on my own. And I told my husband not to put me in his will because that wasn't why I married him." She wouldn't change Callista's mind about her, but maybe if she delayed long enough, someone would figure out she was gone and track her down. Hopefully, before she died. The slim chance was all she had.

Callista's eyes watered. "He was my everything. He kept me safe from Dad. And when Dad tried to rape me, Brian stopped him and from then on slept in my bed to protect me."

Susan couldn't imagine it. "How old was Brian?"

"Fifteen. He loved me. Nobody loved me as much as him."

He seduced his little sister and they called that love? It was only a step up from rape.

Susan hadn't really believed that Callista was California, but now it made a sick kind of sense.

"Whose idea was it for Brian to find a rich wife?" Even a few more minutes of life were worth fighting for.

"His. He said he could kill her without suspicion if he was married a year. But all those rich bitches at the other golf clubs only dated him a short while before breaking up with him. But you"—she pointed an accusing finger at Susan—"the woman who only looked like she was rich, had to fall for him. And spoil everything."

"Then why didn't he divorce me?" It would have saved a lot of lives.

"He got used to all the extras, like that Lexus and the mansion."

Susan had sold Brian's car two weeks after his death, not wanting the reminder. It seemed that living in wealth was more important to Brian than his sister-slash-lover.

"I'm sorry this all happened to you, but killing me isn't going to help. It won't bring him back. It won't make you feel better."

Callista slapped Susan's cheek, and her eyes watered from the sting. "It won't bring him back, but it will make me feel better to know the woman who caused his death is dead."

Susan wouldn't be able to change the mad woman's mind, but talking added more minutes to her life, and gave Autumn a better chance to reach the office and be safe from Callista. If only Gary was trying to find her, but that was too much to hope for. "If Brian hadn't killed all those women, he wouldn't have been arrested. He wouldn't have had to worry about going to prison."

As Callista's hand swung toward her, Susan braced herself to not be flung from the chair. That would probably mean her instant death. Her head whipped to the side when the hand connected with her cheek in another hard slap. Susan took shallow breaths, willing the pain to subside.

"He didn't kill them!" Callista poked a thumb at her own chest. "Brian saved me from being raped. He wouldn't rape another woman."

How could this woman be so delusional? "He loved you. Those other women didn't mean anything to him. He had a woman tied up and was seconds from raping her. How much more evidence does there need to be?"

"A good lawyer would have proved his innocence." She pointed a finger. "But you wouldn't hire one. He knew a public defender couldn't beat the charge, so he did what you forced him into. You're responsible for taking Brian away from me."

Susan didn't know if Callista meant she'd taken Brian by marrying him or by not saving him from suicide. It didn't matter. Help wasn't coming, and now it was her time to die.

"Stand up."

Susan stayed seated, waiting to see Callista's response.

The woman snatched the knife off the counter and held it to Susan's stomach, pricking her skin.

"I can stab this in a couple of times and twist. I hear gut wounds are pretty painful. And slow."

It wasn't a choice she thought she'd ever have to make—bloody intestines spilling out of her or a broken neck. If Gary ended up being one of the people to find her, she didn't want him to see her blood all over. With her hands tied behind her back, she couldn't fight. She got to her feet, but Callista didn't move back far enough, so the knife dug in a little. Probably not even enough to need stitches. Not that it mattered.

"Kneel on the chair."

She complied.

"Now stand on it."

This was it. She'd be dead in the next few minutes. At least Autumn was away from here and maybe had reached Susan's office already. She'd never see her again. Or Gary, or Theo and Bradley. They'd take care of Autumn. And it would be nothing like the way Brian had taken care of his sister. Susan couldn't hold back the tears, but she wouldn't sob. This woman wouldn't get the satisfaction of seeing her emotional pain.

She closed her eyes, imagining Gary and Autumn hugging like they had at the lake, as Callista retied the rope on the door handle, pulling it against her neck.

Chapter 13

Gary slowed as he passed Susan's office. This was the route the bus took, and it probably stayed on the main street for a while, but where did Susan get off? He had no way of knowing until he heard from Chris. He didn't want to keep driving and get too far away, but the location had been far enough that she couldn't have walked.

He drove at a crawl, glad it was a four lane street so cars could pass.

"What are you looking for?" Luke asked.

"Nothing in particular. I'm waiting for Chris's call. Susan wouldn't have boarded a bus just to get off a couple blocks later."

He blinked. A kid walked on the sidewalk. It shouldn't be, but he was fairly sure it was Autumn. He pulled to the curb and jumped out. Her cheeks were flushed as if she'd been running, and her breath came in short gasps. He raced to her, giving her a hug. "Autumn, you're safe."

She wrapped her arms tightly around his waist, her body trembling.

The other door of the car opened, and Luke came up beside them.

Autumn tipped her head back, tears streaking her face. "Gary, the bad lady has Mom." She sucked in a quavering breath. "Sh-she's going to kill her." Autumn buried the side of her head in Gary's stomach. "She made me leave."

Gary thanked God that the kidnapper had released Autumn. She'd been a courageous girl to walk away and get this far, however far it was.

He bent, taking her hands in his, and stared her straight in the eye. "Luke and I are going to do our best to save your mom. Can you lead us back to her?" He didn't want Autumn to go back to the place she'd escaped from, but if it got them to the location faster than waiting for Chris's call, all the better for Susan.

She nodded and bit her lip. "I think so."

He rushed her back to the car. "Here. You sit in front."

Luke got in behind them, and Gary pulled back onto the road.

"Mom said to go right, right and left. And I did it right because I found you."

He patted her hand, relieved she *had* found him. She could have gone the wrong way and gotten in more trouble. "You sure did."

"The bad lady hurt Chris, too."

"Chris is okay. He called to tell me the lady took you. Honey, do you know which street you came from?"

"I walked a long way." Her lip trembled as she stared out the window.

A kid's long walk might not seem so far in the car. She pointed out the window. "I passed that dog on the porch." The sad animal lay with its head on its paws.

"You're doing great. What else looks familiar?"

They passed another street corner. "I saw that tricycle." It was abandoned beside cement steps.

So far, they hadn't driven too far. He wished they could get there faster. Susan might not have much time. He couldn't rush Autumn or she might panic, then it would take that much longer to find Susan. He needed to keep her in search mode and her mind off her mother.

"And all those papers blown into the fence."

"You've got a great memory, Autumn."

They crossed another corner, and another. He hoped they hadn't missed where Susan got off the bus. Her life might hinge on the memory of a scared little girl.

Autumn pointed. "I saw that, too." She indicated an old-fashioned barbershop pole. She didn't say anything for a couple more blocks.

Gary worried they'd run out of distinctive details to keep her on track. She'd done better than he expected, but they were closer to the house and she must have been more panicked when she first left.

"There! It's a lost dog sign. I came from that way." She pointed down a street.

Gary turned right. "How far?"

"Um, two blocks?"

His phone rang and he answered. "What have you got, Chris?"

"Here's the address where my car is." He rattled off the number and street. The street they were coming up on.

"Thanks, Chris." He slipped the phone back into his pocket. He had a great little guide who got him here faster, but verification was good.

Autumn leaned forward, staring through Gary's window. "There. That house with the long grass." More tears ran down her cheeks. "Mom's in there."

Chris's car was parked in front of the house next to it. Hopefully they were in time to rescue Susan. He pulled to the curb two houses short and on the opposite side of the road from the house.

Gary hugged Autumn. "You did great. Where in the house are they?"

"The kitchen." Autumn put a hand on her throat. "She put a rope around Mom's neck."

He caught his breath, and his chest tightened. Susan might be dead already. He couldn't think like that. This was a rescue, the most important one he'd ever do. "Now, I need you to scrunch down on the floor until Luke, or I, or a uniformed police officer comes to get you. I'll lock the doors when I get out." He hated leaving her alone, but Susan's chances were better with Luke helping him.

She unbuckled and slid to the floor. She blinked several times, tears squeezing out, and she wiped them away. "Save Mom."

"I'll do my best." Her distress cut deep and he had to pull in a long breath to get into police mode. He and Luke exited and locked the car. Gary called Luke so they'd have an open line and put his phone on speaker, then pocketed it. "I'll let you know when I'm at the back door, then we'll both shoot the locks and kick the doors in."

He hoped it went as easy as that. Callista, California, or whoever she was, could have a gun, and that would be riskier.

Gary headed to the side of the house. He ducked down when passing windows. At the back stairs, he took care placing each foot over the stringer in case the steps creaked. He pulled his gun, clicked off the safety then tipped his head to get closer to his phone. "I'm in position. Go."

Gary threw back the storm door, and shot the lock a second after Luke. He held onto the storm door for more leverage and kicked the door. It flew open, and a flash of movement caught his eye.

Susan dropped a foot, her toes brushing the floor. A rope wrapped around her neck and extended to a hook in the ceiling, then to the door. He raced to her and lifted her. It might already be too late. He couldn't think that. She had to survive. For Autumn. For him.

California attacked him—kicking and hitting. "Let her die! She deserves to die for Brian."

Luke dashed in, grabbed the mad woman and pushed her to the floor. He cuffed her hands behind her back, then hurried to the back door and slipped the knot off the handle lever, loosening the rope. He came over and yanked it through the hook. "Lower her down, now."

Gary placed Susan on the floor and took the rope from her neck. He checked for respiration and pulse, but didn't find them. With her hands behind her back, he couldn't lay her flat for CPR. He looked around frantically and his eye caught on a knife lying on the counter. He grabbed it and cut the rope, freeing her hands. He started chest compressions as Luke called for an ambulance and police cruiser. He shifted to rescue breathing, then back to compressions. She might have been without oxygen for too long, but he wouldn't give up. "Come on, honey. You have to be okay. Autumn needs you. I need you."

Back to mouth-to-mouth. Switching to chest compressions, he raised his voice. "Susan, please. Breathe!"

He switched between breathing into her mouth and compressing her chest. Each time he had a chance, he begged her to breathe.

Susan gasped in a breath—the sweetest sound Gary had ever heard. He touched her neck and found a good solid heartbeat.

He kissed her cheek and forehead. "Honey, you're safe. Everything's okay now."

Her eyes fluttered open and she stared at him for endless seconds. He hoped she hadn't suffered brain damage.

"Gary. Autumn. She's lost."

He winced at her raspy voice.

"No. I found her."

Susan struggled to sit and he dragged her onto his lap, hugging her. His eyes misted and he blinked to clear them.

Susan touched his cheek. "You're crying."

He buried his head in her shoulder. "I thought I lost you."

She rubbed the back of his neck. "You saved me. And Autumn."

He stood with her in his arms. "Let me take you into the other room and I'll go get her." He didn't want her anywhere near California. He glanced at Luke. "You good here?"

"I've got this."

Gary set Susan on the other side of the wall. At least this floor was carpeted. "I'll be right back."

"Wait. Gary, I love you. Thank you." Her eyes watered. He wasn't sure if it was from the pain of speaking or the stress of almost dying and fearing for her daughter.

He grinned. "I love you, too. I'll be right back."

He raced out the front door as a police car pulled up, lights flashing. He rounded his car and beeped the car locks then opened the passenger door. He gathered up Autumn. "I found her and she's safe now."

Autumn threw her arms around Gary's neck. "I was so scared. You saved her."

"Hey, you saved her. I wouldn't have gotten here in time except you remembered how to get back. You're the hero. Let's go see your mom."

He carried her into the house as the ambulance stopped out front, and set her on the floor near the door. Susan leaned against the wall, and Autumn ran to her, snuggling into her lap. He had things he should take care of, but he sat down beside Susan and wrapped his arms around his beloved girls.

Two paramedics entered, one carrying a large case. Gary waved a hand. "Over here. She was hanging from a rope when I came in." He stood and held his arms out to Autumn. "Come here, sweetheart. Let's let the men check out your mom."

Autumn had been daring and effervescent when she was swimming or at the lake house, but now, she clung to Gary like a toddler. She'd probably thought her bodyguard had died, and who knew what the mad woman had said to her or done before Susan arrived. Leaving the house where her mother had a noose around her neck had to have been heartbreaking for Autumn.

He hugged her tighter. He'd come too close to losing both of them.

One of the paramedics left and came back a minute later with a stretcher.

"I don't need—" Susan whispered.

Gary set Autumn down and squatted beside Susan. "Your heart stopped. I gave you CPR. You're going to the hospital to get every test they think you need."

Her eyes widened.

The paramedics worked together to put a cervical collar on her, then supported her neck as they assisted her onto the gurney.

Gary clasped her shoulder. "We won't be far behind."

The paramedics wheeled her out and Gary stepped into the kitchen doorway. "Luke, do you mind riding back with one of these guys? I'd like to go directly to the hospital now."

Luke waved him off. "Go ahead. I'll handle this."

Gary took Autumn's hand, then led her outside. He opened the back door of his car. "Get in, sweetheart. I'm going to call your brothers so they can meet us at the hospital."

He closed the door so she wouldn't hear the call. He checked the time. Theo should be at work still. Gary dialed AAJ Electronics. He got put through immediately.

"Gary? What's wrong?"

Why else would he call Theo at work? "Susan's all right, but she's on her way to the hospital. Autumn is with me."

"What happened? Why does she need the hospital?"

Gary stepped farther from the car, and gave a brief description of the events, leaving out that Susan had been hanged and technically died. He'd save that for after Theo and Bradley saw Susan, if he ever told them.

"Okay. I'll get Bradley and we'll be on our way. Thanks for letting me know."

"You're welcome."

He got in the car and tried to keep up a lively conversation with Autumn, but it fell flat. She'd been through so much and wanted to be with her mother.

Susan seemed all right, but there could be permanent damage to her neck. The most important thing was that she'd survived, and he was overjoyed.

~~~

Susan closed her eyes, pushing away thoughts of the last time she'd been in a hospital room—the day Anthony died. In a sense, today was a celebration of life. Hers.

An icepack numbed her neck, and she'd had several soothing swallows of cold water. Her eyes watered from uttering two or three words yet still felt like they were full of sand. The doctor had told her blood vessels had burst and it would take a few days for them to feel better. Every breath hurt, not just her throat, but her ribs from the CPR.

She was waiting for more testing to check the extent of the injury to her neck and throat, and the best hope was that it could take weeks for her to recover.

She'd died.

If Gary had arrived a couple of minutes later, she wouldn't be here. All the pain didn't compare to not surviving. Autumn still had her mother. That was more important to her than any discomfort she suffered.

The doctor had informed her that since her heart had stopped, she would stay overnight for observation. At least the threat was gone. Crazy Callista was no longer a menace.

Gary walked into her room and grinned, Autumn beside him, their hands clasped. Today had sealed their bond for good.

He lifted Autumn onto the bed next to her. Susan wrapped her arms around her daughter, and didn't want to let go. Gary leaned down and kissed her forehead, then her daughter's. Susan held up her hand and he gripped it.

He whispered, "I love you. I was terrified today."

He turned at a commotion in the hall, and Theo and Bradley walked in. They stepped to the opposite side as the icepack slipped. Both their gazes landed on her neck, and their eyes widened. Obviously, no one had told them what had happened. She pushed the pack back into place.

Autumn stood on the bed. "Theo! Bradley!" Theo was the closest, and she flung herself at him. He caught and hugged her.

Gary patted the bed. "Autumn, why don't you sit with your mom while I talk to your brothers? It hurts her throat to talk, so if she starts to say something, do this." He touched his index finger to Susan's lips.

She was tempted to purse her lips and kiss his finger, but with everyone looking at her, she didn't.

Autumn stared at Susan. "Okay."

~~~

Gary led the brothers a short distance down the hallway. He didn't want Autumn to hear him.

Theo crossed his arms. "What happened?"

Gary explained how Chris was taken down, the security guard's call, and finding Autumn. "If not for her good memory to get us back to the house, we would have been too late to save Susan." He rubbed a hand over his eyes. "As it was, I had to administer CPR because her heart had stopped." He never wanted to experience that again.

"Jeez," Theo said. Both men had paled.

Bradley touched his neck. "She was choked?"

"Callista Jeffers put a noose around her neck and hanged her."

Bradley leaned his back against the wall and closed his eyes. "This is unbelievable. She's as crazy as her brother."

Theo gripped Gary's shoulder. "Thanks for saving her."

"A joint effort. Autumn's more the hero than me."

A nurse passed with an empty wheelchair and turned into Susan's room.

"They must be doing more tests," Gary said. "Why don't

you two take Autumn home and I'll call you later with results?"

The brothers exchanged a look and nodded. The three returned to Susan's room. The nurse was helping her into the chair while Autumn watched.

Theo rested his arm around Autumn's shoulders. "Autumn, why don't we go home and let the doctors and nurses help your mom get better?"

"But—"

"When they're done testing, she'll want to sleep. Just like you when you're sick. She'll get better faster if she can rest."

"Okay." Autumn slid off the bed and hugged Susan. "Bye, Mom."

Susan nodded. Her throat must be really bad if she didn't speak to her daughter.

The three left and Gary patted Susan's shoulder. "I'll wait here for you."

The nurse whisked her into the hall.

Gary called Luke. "Did you get her booked?"

"Yeah. Her name doesn't check out."

"Did she give you California Jackson?"

"Yes."

"The ID was fake. Try Callista Jeffers." He wasn't one-hundred-percent sure, but it was likely.

Luke whistled. "Jeffers' sister?"

"Yes. As far as I can tell, they were lovers."

"Man, that's twisted. No wonder the woman is crazy. We're setting her up for a psych eval."

"Can you bring a laptop when you come to question Susan? She can't talk, so I figured she could type her statement."

"Good idea. I'll probably be a half-hour."

"Oh. And can you bring a notepad and pen to leave with her?" Gary didn't know how long Susan's throat would be affected, but he wanted to make it as easy as possible for her.

"Will do. See you later."

Gary sat in the chair beside the bed. All the precautions

he'd taken and he still hadn't been able to protect Susan or Autumn.

Chapter 14

Susan relaxed in the hospital bed, the head raised, and her hand in Gary's. He poured more ice water into her cup. She couldn't stop sipping the cool, soothing liquid.

A man in jeans and a button-down shirt walked in carrying a laptop case and Susan's purse. He was the officer who questioned her about Brian's car when they were searching for the serial killer. She'd thought surely coincidence was the only reason Brian's car matched the one they searched for.

Gary stood. "Susan, this is Lieutenant Luke Cade, our lead detective. He brought a laptop so you can write your statement."

She nodded. She couldn't imagine trying to talk through her whole experience.

Luke placed her purse on the bed beside her. "This was at the scene. We had to clear it before returning it."

He took out the laptop and placed it on her tray. He turned it on, then faced it toward her with a blank document page. Next, he pulled out a yellow notepad and pen and set them beside her purse. "These are for you."

She nodded again.

Luke patted the laptop. "I want you to type up what happened from the time Callista Jeffers contacted you. I'll read it over and ask any questions I might have."

Her fingers hovered over the keys as she composed the first words. The fear she felt when she saw the text from Autumn's phone and the picture would forever be seared in her mind. The thought reminded her that Autumn's bodyguard had been attacked.

She picked up the paper and wrote, *How is Chris?* And turned it to face Gary.

"He's fine. Callista tased him. He's angry that he wasn't suspicious of her, but she came out of the school behind them."

She made an okay gesture and rested her fingers on the keyboard. She started typing about the text she received and continued up to Callista yanking the chair out from under her. She didn't write about the terror of her airflow being cut off, or the intense pressure in her eyes, or the last thoughts she had before her world went dark.

The words in front of her wavered, and she glanced up at the *pfft* of Gary pulling a tissue from the box beside the laptop. He sat on the bed and wiped the tears she hadn't realized had fallen. His arms came around her. "I am so sorry this happened to you. You and Autumn are safe now."

Luke stepped forward. "Let's see what you've written." Without turning the laptop, he leaned in and read her words, and Gary read from Susan's other side.

Gary's arm tightened around her. She hadn't been able to tell him the scary events.

"Their father must have been psycho, too," he said.

That could be what happened to the siblings. Brian and Callista had inherited some kind of mental illness gene from their father. Or maybe the two would have turned out differently if their father had gone to prison for murdering the oldest brother. No way to know now.

Luke rested a hand on her shoulder. "Thanks, Susan. This will help with our interrogation of Callista. If you think of anything you missed, call…text me. I'll print this back at the office, and Gary can get it to you to sign." He set a card on the table with his number on it. He closed the laptop, and rubbed the back of his neck. "I'm glad you made it. It didn't look good when I first entered that house."

She held her hand out and he clasped it, patting it with his other hand.

He scooped up his laptop, and waved. "See you tomorrow, Gary."

"Thanks for coming with me, Luke. I couldn't have done it alone," Gary said.

Moments after Luke left, the doctor walked in with a tablet in hand, and stopped beside her bed. "All the tests look good. Your brain scan was normal. No bleeding or dark spots. And there's no permanent damage to your throat."

She grinned.

He shook a finger. "No talking for three days. And sparingly after that for a while. It'll probably hurt for a couple of weeks. I checked the history on your heart monitor and it reads normal, too."

"Thank you, doctor," Gary said.

"And you are?"

"Susan's boyfriend, Detective Gary Wassman."

She wrote on her notepad and showed the doctor. *He's the one who performed CPR on me.*

The doctor's eyebrows rose. "Detective, you saved her life."

Gary gripped Susan's hand and stared into her eyes. "I couldn't lose her."

"I'll check on you in the morning," the doctor said before he left.

Gary pushed a chair into the corner. "I'm going to sack out over here."

She shook her head, and wrote on her paper. *You don't have to stay. The Dr said I'm OK.*

He sat on the edge of the bed and kissed her forehead. "You were traumatized today. You nearly died. You thought

Autumn would die. I'll be here for you in case you have bad dreams."

Her eyes misted and she blinked so tears wouldn't fall. She mouthed, 'Thank you,' then wrote again. *Can you call Theo and see how Autumn is?*

"Yes, of course." Gary pulled out his phone. "I have to update him on your condition anyway." He selected Theo's name and relayed what the doctor said, then inquired about Autumn.

He pocketed his phone and covered her hand. "Theo's been sitting in her room and went out to the hall to talk to me. He's got a sleeping bag on Autumn's floor to spend the night."

She nodded. Autumn's brothers would take care of her. She scanned the room but didn't see her purse. Again she wrote. *Can you text Theo and ask him to have Autumn stay home from school tomorrow?*

"All right. And I'll ask him to call your office in the morning to tell them you won't be in for a few days."

Theo was flexible enough that he could watch Autumn and go into work after Susan got home. Her daughter needed to be with family after her experience. Especially, so she could spend time with Susan, and see for herself that all was well.

~~~

Early morning light crept between the slats of the window blind. Gary stretched and massaged his neck. Spending the night in a hospital chair could almost be considered torture. If the nurse hadn't given him a pillow and blanket, it would have been worse.

Susan's hoarse cries had woken him once in the night, and he'd talked and soothed her through it. He hoped they hadn't made her worse this morning. He was relieved he'd been where she needed him.

A nurse bustled in, and Susan's eyes fluttered open.

He joined them and took Susan's hand as she smiled.

The nurse wrapped a blood pressure cuff around Susan's arm. "How are you feeling this morning?"

Susan touched her throat, and he wondered if she'd tried to talk or if the pain was already too great.

The nurse patted her arm and pumped up the cuff. "Sorry, dear." She noted the results and stored the cuff, then checked her other vitals. Before she left, she said, "I suggest you don't eat the toast when they bring in your breakfast."

Susan grimaced.

Gary took advantage of the empty room and kissed her—careful not to put any strain on her neck. "Good morning."

She wrapped her arms around his neck and buried her face under his ear. Pulling back, she pointed to her notepad on the tray table that had been pushed away. He dragged the table back to the bed, and she picked up the pen. *Thank you for being here last night when I had my nightmare.*

"You're welcome. I wouldn't have been anywhere else." He hugged her. "When I rushed into that house and saw you, I thought I'd lost you," he choked out. "If Luke hadn't come with me, I would have had to fight Callista before I could take you down." He pulled her closer. "I don't think—" His throat tightened up.

Susan grabbed his head and tugged it down. She kissed his wet cheeks.

She pulled back, her beautiful eyes staring into his, and whispered. "I'm alive because of you. Alive!"

The doctor walked in, and Gary didn't care that the man saw him crying. The woman he loved was alive, and that was all that mattered. He plucked a tissue from the box on Susan's table and wiped his cheeks.

The doctor gently probed Susan's neck. "The medication has reduced the swelling." He shone a light into her mouth and used a tongue depressor. "Swelling's down in your throat, too."

He dropped the stick in the trash and stuck the light into his pocket. "You're one lucky woman."

Lucky would have been not being hanged. Lucky would have been not being kidnapped, or not being stalked, or not marrying a serial killer, or not having her husband die so young. She'd been unlucky for so long and in so many ways that it was time for her luck to change.

"I'll start the paperwork for your release, and by the time you've eaten breakfast, you should be good to go."

"Thank you, doctor," Gary said.

After the doctor left, Susan wrote on her paper. *Will you stay with me?*

He cupped the side of her head. "I'm not going anywhere."

She shook her head and wrote. *Come home with me. Stay with us.*

"I'll be with you as much as you need me. You want me to stay over?"

She wrote a message. *In my bed?*

He stared into her eyes. "As much as I want that, I think Autumn needs you more. How about if I stay in a guest room?"

She smiled and hugged him.

~~~

It was noon by the time Gary walked into Luke's office, and sat in the chair in front of his desk. "Susan's home. Theo is staying until I get back."

Luke nodded. "You're taking some time off?"

"Yeah. I'm taking a few days. How did Callista's questioning go?"

"She's one crazy woman. We got all we need to prosecute, but I don't think she'll be released from the hospital once the psych eval is completed."

Gary breathed a long sigh. "I don't care how they keep her

as long as she can't get to Susan again."

"How's Autumn?"

"She's okay. Theo said she only woke up crying once in the night. She sure was happy to see her mom."

Luke clenched his hands. "It's amazing how being held captive for a couple hours by a crazed killer can have such long-lasting effects. Shannon still has the occasional nightmare."

Luke's wife had been Jeffers' last victim. Gary understood even more now how Luke had felt the day she almost died.

Luke stood and squeezed Gary's shoulder. "Make sure they both talk to a therapist. It made all the difference for Shannon."

Gary rose and shook his friend's hand. "I'll do that. And thanks again for yesterday."

Luke gave him a half hug. "I'm glad I was there for you." His friend's penetrating stare said more than any words could.

Gary picked up clothes at his house before heading back to Susan's. He parked in the additional space to the right of the garage, then went to the front door with his bag.

Theo answered the bell, glanced at the bag, but didn't mention it. "Let me give you the garage door code so you can come in on your own. It works on both doors and the security panel." He recited four digits. "Susan and Autumn are in the living room."

"All right. Thanks."

Theo glanced at his watch. "Now, I have to get to the office. I have a meeting this afternoon that couldn't be cancelled."

"See you later." Gary dropped his bag beside the door and followed Autumn's voice into the nearest room.

Susan sat in the corner of a couch with Autumn snuggled beside her. Autumn looked up from the *Harry Potter* book she was reading aloud, then dropped the book beside her. "Gary!"

He strode across the space, and propped his hands on the couch back and arm, then kissed both his girls on the forehead. He met Susan's gaze. "You okay?"

She nodded and wrote on her paper. *Autumn's been asking to swim, but I'm not up to it. Can you?*

He grinned. "I'd love to. Autumn, do you want to swim?"

Autumn scrambled up. "Yay! I'll go change." She raced out of the room.

He noticed the way Susan's eyes drooped. "Do you want to take a nap?"

She scribbled her note. *I'll come watch.*

Susan made a come here gesture. He leaned in and she wrapped her arms around his neck, giving him a kiss. She tipped her head back and whispered. "I love you."

His heart squeezed. He'd been so close to never hearing those words again. He pulled her to her feet and into his arms. "I love you so much." Gary didn't want to let go, but he had something important to do. "I've got to get changed before Autumn comes back down." He grabbed his bag from beside the front door and they strolled to the pool room. Gary settled Susan on a lounge chair, and adjusted an umbrella over her to block the glare of the mid-morning sun. In a changing room, he put on his swim trunks. Before he returned, Autumn's voice carried through the door.

"Mom, are you going to marry Gary?"

Unfortunately, he couldn't hear Susan's response. It sounded like Autumn wouldn't be opposed.

He joined the girls. "Autumn, you ready for that swim? Do you want to race?"

"Yes!" She race-walked to the end of the pool. Apparently, she'd been told enough times not to run around the pool.

He kissed Susan's forehead. "I'd ask you to call 'go', but it's against doctor's orders."

He joined Autumn at the pool edge. "Call it, Autumn."

She bent forward, ready to dive in. Her words rushed out. "One-two-three-go."

She splashed in before Gary, but he passed her easily. He kept a little ahead, encouraging her to gain a bit more speed than last time. He checked her form, and once corrected, she started to gain on him. He made sure they finished with a tie.

Gary grabbed a ball from a basket beside the pool and they tossed it around for a bit, until he called a stop. "One more race, then it's time to change."

"Aw."

He lifted Autumn out of the pool and boosted himself up beside her. They raced once again, and this time Gary won by a foot.

She scrambled up the ladder. "See you soon."

Gary joined Susan, only to find she'd gone to sleep. He showered and dressed then sat in the chair next to hers. He recalled Autumn's question and slipped Susan's notepad out from under her leg. A blank page. He flipped the previous page back. *We'll see, honey.*

She hadn't said no.

Chapter 15

Susan stretched and dropped her hand onto the bed beside her. Gary was gone, and the shower wasn't running, so likely he'd left. The night before, he'd said he wanted to check in at the station in the morning but would be back.

Autumn had slept in Susan's bed the first night Susan was home and after that, insisted she was fine in her own room.

They'd visited a therapist the day before. It would have been easier to do once she could talk again, but Susan didn't want Autumn to suffer for days if this was what she needed. It took longer since all her responses had to be written, but the therapist repeated most of it back anyway, so Autumn didn't have to read it, too. They'd had a two-hour session beginning with them talking with the therapist together then Autumn spent a short time alone with the therapist followed by Susan. During her time, the therapist told Susan that Autumn seemed well adjusted after the ordeal. She credited Gary for emphasizing that he wouldn't have been able to rescue Susan without Autumn's help. It aided her in overcoming the powerlessness she'd felt while being a captive.

Three days had passed quickly with Gary by her side. She'd expected to be bored being home so long, but talking with Gary through a laptop and spending time floating in the pool or in the hot tub, was a vacation.

Today, Susan would try her voice out, but first, a hot shower might loosen it up. She rolled out of bed and showered, then dried her hair. She tipped her head up and gently touched her neck. The redness was gone, but the bruising was darker. Touching it or turning her head still hurt, but the constant ache in her throat was gone.

Now to test the regular volume of her voice. "I love Gary."

His voice from the other room startled her. "I love you, too."

She leaned against the doorframe and crossed her arms. "I didn't hear you come in." It still hurt to talk, and her voice showed it, but it didn't bring tears to her eyes as it had initially.

"I got back while you were drying your hair." He wrapped his arms around her and kissed her. "I brought breakfast." He gestured to a tray on the bed.

"Mmm. Thank you." That strained her throat more than before. Maybe she should avoid talking for a while.

She went to her dresser.

"You don't have to get dressed yet. Just climb back under the covers."

She looked him up and down then whispered. "You're dressed."

He grinned and yanked his shirt over his head. "I can fix that."

By the time she was under the covers, he had his clothes off and set the tray over her lap. He climbed in beside her.

Two takeout cups of coffee sat in the corners. She lifted the cover of one container. "Oh, crepes." She picked up a slice of strawberry and scooped it into whipped cream.

"There's this restaurant near the station. Sorry they're no longer hot, but still warm and taste good." He opened the other container, and handed her a fork.

They ate in silence, preserving her throat on her part. Once the tray was empty of food, Gary set it on the floor. "Now, what do you want to do?"

Susan pulled him down with her. With how hoarse her voice was, she hoped her whispers were sexy. "I want to make love. You've been in bed with me for two nights, and it's driving me crazy."

He dropped gentle kisses on her neck. "Do you think you're up to it? I can tell your throat still hurts."

"Maybe I'll try not to enjoy myself too much."

"I'll have to make sure you fail at that." He kissed her lips. "I love you."

"I love you, too."

He'd shown her in so many ways how much he loved her. Even without the words she wouldn't doubt it.

His lips and hands caressed her body, building her need for him, and pushing any thoughts but the two of them out of her mind. Her bliss increased, and she kneaded his shoulders. So far, she'd been able to keep silent, but her quickened breathing caused some throat strain. It was worth it. He slid up her body and kissed her as he surged into her. He filled her. Filled her life. Filled her heart.

In moments she tumbled over the edge, followed by Gary. She'd nearly succeeded in not making a sound.

He turned them on their sides and ran a hand up and down her spine as they caught their breaths.

He kissed her neck. "Your throat must be dry after that. I'll get you some water."

"No. It's—"

He was propped up on his hands. "I'll be right back."

Water ran in the bathroom and he returned shortly with a full glass.

She sat up. "Thank you."

He winced. Her throat was more irritated than earlier.

She gulped down the soothing drink, and set the glass on the side table. "I don't regret what we just did, so don't get ideas that this is your fault."

He climbed into bed, leaned against the headboard and pulled her into his arms. "A few days ago, I found out how devastated I would be without you in my life."

She snuggled her head into the side of his neck. "I can't imagine mine without you either." She wouldn't be here to enjoy their time together without his rescue. She flipped around, straddling him, placing a hand on each side of his face. "I will forever be grateful that you saved my life for Autumn's sake."

He opened his mouth, and she covered it with her fingers.

"But—" She kissed his nose since his mouth wasn't available. "—I love you for you. Your kind heart, the way you care about Autumn, the way you show me that you love me. I didn't think I'd find this kind of love again. I thought I would forever have a piece missing from my heart, but you filled it perfectly."

Gary tugged her hand away from his mouth. "You did the same for me. Please marry me, Susan."

Her mouth dropped open, as he stared into her eyes. She thought, eventually, they might get married, but she was surprised he was sure already. No, she shouldn't be surprised. He'd cried when he told her how he almost lost her. Gary was a man who loved deeply, just like Anthony had. She could trust this love.

"Yes. Forever, yes."

He opened the nightstand drawer and pulled out a small box. Her breath caught. It wasn't spur of the moment. He'd planned to ask her.

Behind her back, the box creaked open, then plopped onto the bed. He brought his hands between them and took hers. She stared down where they were linked, and when he did nothing more, she looked into his eyes. They twinkled as he slid a ring onto her finger and kissed her.

She glanced down. It was beautiful, an oval cut solitaire— just the right size. She threw her arms around him. "I love it."

He lay back down with her beside him and kissed her forehead. "I don't want a long engagement."

"Me neither. And I want a small, quiet wedding."

He scooted back and squinted. "Are you sure? I thought women liked big weddings."

"Gary, this will be my third wedding." Not that she wanted to remind him she'd been married twice before—and both husbands were dead. "But I know this is your first, so if you want a big wedding, I'll go along with it."

"Nope. You, me, close family, and a few friends are all I need."

"Okay. My necessaries are Autumn, Theo, and Bradley."

"Mine will be my sister, niece, and Luke."

Susan kissed him then laid her head on his chest. "I thought I'd have only one true love, and I was destined to be alone." She lifted her upper body and stared into Gary's compassionate eyes. "But you proved that wrong. I love you so much."

Gary ran his hand up her arm and rested it against the side of her head. "My heart is filled with love for you—you and Autumn. It started the first time I saw you."

She shivered. She'd still been married then and overwhelmed with the devastating news he'd given her.

Gary kissed her cheek. "You were so strong, defending your husband until I supplied the proof. But you didn't break down. You requested to talk to him yourself." He rubbed his thumb on her cheek. "In that moment, I wished I'd met you before he did."

She did, too. That chapter of her life was over, finishing with a big 'The End'. She couldn't ask for anything more than to be surrounded by the people she loved and who loved her. Well, maybe…

Susan smiled. "What do you think of children with the last name of Wassman?"

Gary froze for a second then flipped them so he was on top of her. "I would love to have babies with you. I'm sure Autumn would like younger siblings. Now would be a perfect time to start."

She couldn't agree more.

The End

The description of the third book of the **Choice** series, *No Choice*.

Can no choice be the right choice?

Jessalyn Waters can't believe her brother *sold* her to pay a debt. When he delivers her to the buyer, she fears she'll be forced to become a sex slave.

Theo Argyle did the only thing he could to protect Jessalyn. He paid off the debt. Fearing for her safety, he demands she be brought to him, then coerces her into marriage.

Jessalyn is given no choice, and she'll remind Theo every chance she gets, even though everything he does is to protect her. The last thing she should do is fall for him, but his charm is impossible to resist.

Can Theo keep Jessalyn safe and convince her that they belong together even after the danger is vanquished?

Books by Deborah Wallace

Wounded Warrior Hearts Series (Clean Romance)
Wounded Warrior Hearts: Steven
Wounded Warrior Hearts: Amy
Wounded Warrior Hearts: Russ

Rawlins Series (Paranormal Romance – witches)
Kathleen's Legacy
Jason's Forbidden Woman
Jamie's Trials
Adam's Redemption
Kristy's Puzzle
Tony's to Protect
Abby's Salem Legacy
Keith's Return
Gabe's Atonement – *December 2024*

Choice Series (Romantic Suspense)
Second Choice
Third Choice
No Choice
Her Choice
Series complete

Unknown Series (Romantic Suspense)
Father Unknown
Killer Unknown
Series complete

Other Books (Romantic Suspense)
I Shot the Sheriff
Your Love Belongs to Me
Summer Love

Searching for Stephanie
New Memories – You can receive this book free by signing up for my newsletter on my website.

Check out my website for details on these books and where to find them. You can also sign up to receive emails when I have a new book. www.DeborahWallaceBooks.com.

Or find my books on Amazon:
https://www.amazon.com/Deborah-Wallace/e/B07XDL4X89

Thanks for reading. While you're waiting on the next story, if you would be so kind as to leave a review for this book, that would be wonderful. I appreciate the feedback and support. Reviews lift my spirits and boost my creativity. Thank!

About Deborah Wallace

Deborah Wallace decided to try writing what she liked to read, and stories started filling her head. Writing has become a passion, and she can't go long without touching her keyboard.

She's written in different genres, but the stories she keeps coming back to are her favorite—romantic suspense. The first *Rawlins* book was supposed to be the only paranormal. Then she asked 'what if...' and now children of the first characters and a couple of friends have books.

She wrote her first stories in 2014 but didn't publish until 2019.

Deborah grew up in Michigan, but Massachusetts has been her home for more years than she cares to think about. She loves the history, the museums and antique houses, the seacoast and hiking trails.